FREDDY *Goes To* FLORIDA

Freddy had a song for the animals as they were en route to Florida. It sounded like this:

> The weather grew torrider
>   and torrider,
> And the orange-blossoms smelt
>   horrider and horrider
> As we marched down into Florida.

Between soaking up the sun and annoying the alligators, the party stirred up adventure all along the line and emerged with a bag of gold for Mr. Bean.

To quote everyone who reads it: "This is a very funny book." Kurt Wiese's drawings are not based on the snapshots taken by Freddy in Florida, but they are extremely suitable to the story, to say the least.

Mrs. Wiggins he dotted all over.

FREDDY
Goes to
FLORIDA

---

by Walter R. Brooks

Illustrated by Kurt Wiese

A YEARLING BOOK

To

ANNE AND NANNIE

Published by
Dell Publishing Co., Inc.
1 Dag Hammarskjold Plaza
New York, New York 10017

This book was originally published in 1927 under the title of *To and Again*. This edition was published in February 1949 with new illustrations and title.

Yearling ® TM 913705, Dell Publishing Co., Inc.

ISBN: 0-440-42577-8

Reprinted by arrangement with Alfred A. Knopf, Inc.

Printed in the United States of America

First Yearling printing—April 1980

CW

I

CHARLES, the rooster, came out of the front door of the chicken coop and walked slowly across the barn-yard. It was still very dark in the barn-yard, for it was half past four in the morning, and the sun was not yet up. He shivered and thought of his nice warm perch in the coop, but there was a reason why he did not go back to it. Mr. Bean, the farmer, did not have very much money, and could not afford to buy an alarm-clock, and he relied on the rooster to wake him up bright and early in the morning. The last time Charles had overslept, Mr. Bean had been very angry and had threatened to have him fricasseed with baking-powder biscuit for Sunday dinner. Charles did not like getting up early, before any of the other birds and animals were stirring, but he felt that it was better to get up than to be fricasseed. And so this morning he hopped sleepily on to a post and, after clearing his throat several times, began to crow: "Cock-a-doodle-doo! Cock-a-doodle-doo-oo-oo!!"

The eastern sky grew brighter and brighter and pinker and pinker, and for a long time nothing else happened. Then some robins began talking together in little quiet voices in the big elm-tree that grew by the barn, and a young chipmunk came scampering along the fence and stopped on the post next to Charles and started to wash his face with his paws, and down in the house where the pigs lived there was a great grunting and squealing, so that Charles knew that the pigs were beginning to think about breakfast. And he crowed some more.

And at last, far off across the fields, where the sky came down to meet them, there appeared a little spark of bright gold, that grew and grew until it looked like a bonfire, and then like a house on fire, and then like a whole city burning up. And that was the upper edge of the sun, coming up from the other side of the world, where all night long it had been shining on Chinese pagodas and the Himalayas and jungles in Africa and all the queer places where people work and play while we are sound asleep.

After clearing his throat he began to crow.

And just as the edge of the sun came into sight, the head of Mr. Bean, the farmer, appeared at his bedroom window. He had on a white cotton night-cap with a red tassel, and his face was completely hidden behind his bushy, grey whiskers, so that nobody, not even his wife, had ever seen what he really looked like. And he was looking out to see what kind of a day it was going to be.

As soon as Mr. Bean poked his head out of the window, Charles hopped down from the post. His day's work was already done, but although he was still cold and sleepy, he did not go back to the hen house. For his wife and her eight sisters were up by that time. "And nobody could get a minute's peace in all that cackle," he muttered angrily. "I'll go take forty winks in the barn."

"Good-morning, Charles," said Hank, the old, white horse, whose stall was nearest the door. "Touch of winter in the air this morning."

Charles flew up and perched on the edge of Hank's manger.

"Touch of winter!" he exclaimed. "I guess there is! It's cold, that's what it is—downright cold!"

"Well, we've got to expect it now," said Hank. "Snow will be flying in another month or two."

3

"Ugh!" said Charles, and shivered.

"There's less work for me in winter," said Hank; "though I must say I prefer the summer. I've got a touch of rheumatism in my off hind leg, and these cold nights set it aching."

"Of course," said Charles sympathetically. "They would! It's a shame. You ought to have a blanket or something to cover you, and this barn is a terribly draughty old place. But Mr. Bean, he never thinks how the animals and birds suffer; he sleeps warm under his feather-bed and four patchwork quilts—*he* doesn't care as long as *he's* warm! Now, take me. Every morning, winter and summer, I have to get up before daylight, crawl out of my comfortable coop, and crow and get things started on the farm, just because he's too stingy to buy himself an alarm-clock. Doesn't matter how cold and rainy it is, it has to be done. And if I miss a morning, what do I get? I get fricasseed, that's what!"

"It seems sort of hard," said Hank.

"I guess it does! And now winter's coming. I detest winter! But I've got to get out, just the same, and wade around in the snow and freeze my bill. I wouldn't mind so much if I was warm the rest of the time. If there was a stove in the hen house, and a couple of good wool blankets to sleep under. That hen house ought to have a cellar under it, too—the floor's as cold as stone."

Hank sighed. "Yes," he agreed, "it's a hard life. There's no denying it. But what can we do about it?"

A little twittering voice answered from high up under the roof. "Why don't you migrate?" it said.

They looked up, but it was dark in the roof, and they could not see anything.

"Who are you?" asked Charles. "And what are you talking about?"

"I'm a barn swallow," said the voice, "and I'm talking about migrating. We birds all migrate every year, and I don't see why you can't do it too, if you don't like the winter."

"Oh, you don't!" said Charles rather crossly. "Well, suppose you tell us what you're talking about. If it's worth listening to. We can't keep track of everything you little unimportant birds do."

Charles, being a farm bird, felt very superior to all the wild birds, and he puffed out his chest with

5

importance. But the swallow only laughed chirp-ingly.

"You needn't be so grand," she said. "After all, you've never been outside your own barn-yard, and you have to do as you're told, or you get fricasseed. And I've travelled thousands of miles in my time, and I don't take orders from anyone."

"Well, of all the—!" Charles began angrily. But Hank shook his head at him.

"She may have something interesting to tell us," he said. And then he asked the swallow politely if she would explain to them what migrating was.

So she told them that every fall, when it began to get cold, the birds gathered together in big flocks and started south. They travelled hundreds of miles, and some of them went to Florida, and some went to Central or South America. All winter long, she said, it was sunny and warm down south. There was never any snow, never any cold winds, and there was always plenty to eat. And then in the spring they came back north again.

When she had told them this, she dropped with a twitter from the roof and shot like an arrow out through the open door into the warm sunshine.

"Do you believe it?" Charles asked when she had

6

gone. He felt it beneath his dignity to pay much attention to anything a swallow could tell him, although he was really very much interested.

"Yes," said Hank. "I have heard of it before. And it sounds pretty good. But it wouldn't do for me, I'm afraid. It's a long road to Florida. If I could fly, though, I won't say that I wouldn't try it."

"I can't fly," said Charles. "Not much, that is. But I would walk a good many miles to find a place where it is warm and sunny all winter, and where I shouldn't have to get up in the morning till I got good and ready. It wouldn't be any fun going alone, of course, but if we could get up a party——"

"If you could get up a party," said Hank, "I won't say I shouldn't like to go myself."

Charles jumped down from the manger. "I'm going to see some of the other animals," he said. "If they're interested, we'll have a meeting to-night and talk it over." And he went out into the yard.

The more he thought about it, the more excited he became. He went out into the orchard and talked to an oriole and a couple of blackbirds, and the tales they told him of the lazy life they led in the tropical, southern sunshine fairly made his mouth water. Then he went to see the pigs and the cows and the other animals, and they were very much interested and said that they had all been dreading the long, cold winter, and that if he really knew of a place where it was warm and sunshiny they would be very glad to go there. So he invited them to come to a meeting that evening in the cow barn, where he would tell them all about it, and those who wanted to go could talk it over and decide when to start.

II

NOW, all this time Charles had not said anything to his wife and her eight sisters about what the birds had told him, and he had not invited them to the meeting.

"She always disapproves of everything I do," he grumbled, "and her sisters always agree with her. It will be a much better meeting if she doesn't come. I can tell her about it afterwards." His wife's name was Henrietta, and she was a very busy hen, for she had ten little chickens to take care of. And so she was sometimes rather cross to Charles, who never did much work and used to get in her way a good deal.

That night, when Charles started out, she called him back and asked him where he was going.

"I have to attend a business meeting," he said importantly. "I'm expected to make a speech."

"H'm, much good *your* speech will do anybody!"

said Henrietta; but she was busy putting the chickens to bed, and Charles slipped out before she had time to say any more.

The meeting was a great success. Nearly all the animals on the farm came, and the cow barn was crowded to the doors. Charles spoke long and eloquently and drew glowing pictures of what their life would be like in a southern land, lolling under the orange-trees and telling stories and cracking jokes all day long. The pigs, who had come in a body and sat in the front row, applauded heartily, and the cows mooed and the ducks quacked and the dogs barked, and even the mice, who sat in a row on one of the rafters, squeaked excitedly.

"Now, my friends," said Charles, when he had told them all he had learned from the birds, "I have placed before you these facts. It remains for us to act upon them. I, for one, intend to follow the example of the birds and go south for the winter. It is true that it is easier for the birds than it is for us. The birds can fly across rivers that we shall have to swim or wade, and across mountains that we shall have to climb. I do not conceal from you that it may be a hard journey. But it is my experience that nothing that is worth getting is

The meeting was a great success.

easy to get. However, I shall be glad to hear what anyone else may have to say, and I accordingly throw the meeting open to discussion." And amid prolonged cheers he hopped down from the seat of the old buggy from which he had addressed the meeting.

Then for quite a while the animals were much excited and all talked at once. All of them hated the thought of the long, cold winter, and when somebody—I think it was Freddy, the smallest and cleverest of the pigs—shouted: "Why don't we start to-night?" they all gave three cheers and started toward the door.

But just then Jock, the larger of the two dogs, a wise old Scotch collie, got up.

"Ladies and gentlemen," he began, "you have all heard what my friend the rooster has said, and I think we all agree with him that it would be fine if we could all go south this winter." ("Yes, yes!" cried all the animals together.) "But there is one thing that I think we have forgotten. I am not a fine speaker like Charles, but I just want to say that we must not forget our duty. We cannot all leave Mr. Bean, for he could not get along without us——"

Here Charles interrupted excitedly. "Mr. Bean!" he shouted. "What do we care for Mr. Bean? What has he ever done for us? *He* can sleep warm these winter nights; *he* can have feather-beds and stoves; but *we* don't have such things— *we* don't matter! Why doesn't he warm *our* houses for us? Why——"

"Yes, yes, Charles," said Jock quietly. "But listen to me a minute. Mr. Bean feeds us and gives us a place to live and looks after us when we're sick. We can't just desert him, can we?"

"Well, perhaps you're right," said Charles unwillingly.

"Of course I am," said Jock. And he went on to say that, while those of them whom Mr. Bean did not need during the winter could go south if they wanted to, he thought the others should stay. "I can't go," he said. "And one of the horses should stay to take Mr. Bean into town when he wants to go. And one of the cows and some of the hens ought to stay, too, so he will have eggs and milk. That is all I have to say." And he bowed and sat down.

A long discussion followed, but as all the animals wanted to go, none of them except Jock would admit that they were needed on the farm. They talked louder and louder, and grew more and more angry at each other, and it seemed likely that the meeting would break up in disorder, when there was a loud ear-piercing "Meeaooouw!" and Jinx, the cat, bounded through the doorway.

In the silence that followed, all the mice upon the rafter gave a horrified squeak, and then they rose as one mouse and tiptoed softly into a convenient hole.

"Hello, folks," said Jinx breezily. "What's all the row? I could hear you way down by the mill-pond, where I was hunting frogs. Better make less noise, or you'll have old Bean out here with his shotgun. What's the matter anyway?"

"Fine!" he said when they had told him. "Fine! That's a great idea, Charley, old boy! Didn't think you had it in you. But see here. No use quarrelling about who's to go and who's not. Draw lots; that's the way to do it. Now you say only one cow can go. Well, here's three of 'em—Mrs. Wiggins and Mrs. Wurzburger and Mrs. Wogus. Here, Jock, you take three straws in your mouth, one long one and two short. Now let 'em draw, and the one that gets the long straw goes."

Jock got the straws, and the cows drew. Mrs. Wiggins won.

"All fair and above-board, you see," said Jinx. "Now, horses next. Step up, please; it's getting late."

As soon as the cat had taken charge of things, the meeting became more orderly, and arrangements for the departure of all those whom Mr. Bean would not need during the winter were quickly made. Then, when everything was decided, Charles got up again to make another speech. There wasn't really anything left for him to say, but he was fond of making speeches, and he spoke so beautifully that everybody liked to hear him, although when they got home they could never remember anything he had said.

"Now, my friends," he began, "before we break up this distinguished meeting, I should like to give you one thought to take home with you in your hearts—something to carry away with you as a memento of the kindness and good-fellowship we have enjoyed here together to-night. As I look about me this evening upon all these bright, eager young faces, gathered together here under one roof, it is borne in upon me——" But what it was that was borne in upon him they never knew, for at that point he stopped suddenly and climbed hastily down from the buggy seat. His wife, Henrietta, had come in the door.

She marched straight down toward him between the rows of silent animals, and caught him by the wing.

" 'Bright, eager young faces,' is it?" she exclaimed angrily. "*I'll* give you a bright, eager young face!" And she boxed his right ear with her claw. "*I'll* give you something to carry home with you!" And she boxed the other ear. "I never heard such nonsense!"

Charles hunched his head down between his shoulders. "But, my dear!" he protested.

"Don't you 'my dear' me!" she said. "You come along home, where you belong. Staying out all night like this! Revelling and carousing with a lot of silly pigs and cows that don't know any better! The very idea!" And she pushed him unceremomously toward the door.

But before they reached it another figure appeared—a short. bearded man in a long, white night-shirt and carpet slippers. Mr. Bean had been awakened by the noise, and had come out to see

15

what was the matter. He had a lantern in one hand and a carriage whip in the other, and on his head was the white cotton night-cap with the red tassel.

"You animals go to bed!" he said gruffly. Then he turned round and stumped back to the house.

In thirty seconds all the animals had gone and the cow barn was empty, except for Mrs. Wiggins and Mrs. Wurzburger and Mrs. Wogus, who lived there.

III

THE next morning, as soon as Mr. Bean had left the house, Jinx, the cat, who had been pretending to be asleep under the stove, jumped up on the table and got a pencil and a piece of paper, and carried them out and laid them down under the big elm-tree beside the barn. Then he looked up among the branches, and pretty soon he saw a bright little eye peeping out at him from behind a limb.

"Good-morning, robin," he said politely. "I wonder if you'd do me a little favour? We animals are going to migrate this fall, but as none of us have ever been south before, we don't know the way, and I thought perhaps you'd be willing to draw us a little map."

The robin hopped a little way along the branch and cocked his head and looked down at Jinx with his right eye. "I don't know what made you think that," he said. "I don't know why I should do anything for you. You're always chasing me, and there's never a minute's peace for me or my family when you're in the barn-yard, and you ate up my wife's third cousin last June. But I suppose you've forgotten all about that."

"I certainly haven't," said Jinx. "It was a most regrettable incident, and I was really terribly upset about it. I had no idea that robin was any relative of your wife's, and when I saw him prowling around your nest, I thought he wanted to steal your children, and of course I didn't stop to make inquiries then. Afterwards, when I found out what a mistake I had made, I would have done anything to restore him to you. But of course it was too late."

"Rather late," said the robin dryly, "since there was nothing left of him but a few tail feathers."

"Well, let's not rake up old scores," said Jinx. "What's done is done, as the saying goes. And if you'll make this map for me, I'll promise never to chase you or any of your family again."

"Well, that's fair enough," said the robin. And he flew down, and picking up the pencil in his claw, began to draw the map that would show them exactly how to get to Florida.

Meanwhile all the other animals who were going were packing up and making their farewell calls on those who were to stay at home. For they had heard Mr. Bean say that he was going to drive into town the next morning, and they thought that would be the best time for them to start on their journey, because he wouldn't get back until late in the afternoon, and by that time they would be many miles away.

Nearly everybody in the barn-yard was happy but Charles the rooster. He sat alone in the darkest corner of the hen house, his tail feathers drooping miserably. For his wife, Henrietta, had positively refused to let him go.

"Go south in the winter, would you?" she had said. "Never in my life have I heard such a pack of nonsensical notions! What right have you to go traipsing off over the country—you, with a wife and children to look after? Not that you ever do look after them. Who's going to get Mr. Bean up in the morning, I should like to know?"

"He can wake himself up," said Charles. "He

doesn't have to get up so early in the winter-time anyway."

"Well, you're not going—that's flat!" said his wife. And that settled it. When Henrietta put her foot down, there was nothing more to be said.

Some of the animals, too, had held the opinion that the cat ought not to go either, since it was his duty to keep the mice out of the barn where the grain and vegetables were stored. But that was easily arranged, for some of the mice wanted to go, and so Jinx promised that he would let them alone if the mice that stayed home would keep away from the barn while he was gone. This pleased the other animals, for although Jinx was a wild fellow, rather careless of appearances and a bit too free in his speech, they all felt that he would be a good animal to have with them in a pinch, and no one knew what dangers might lie in wait for them on the road to Florida.

Indeed, a number of the more timid animals who had been carried away by enthusiasm at the meeting in the cow barn had not felt so anxious to go when they had thought it all over. All the sheep had backed out, and most of the mice, and all of the pigs except Freddy. The pigs were not afraid;

they were just awfully lazy, and the thought of walking perhaps twenty miles a day for goodness knew how many days was too much for them.

At last the great day came. Mr. Bean harnessed up William to the buggy early in the morning, and drove off to town, and then all the animals gathered in the barn-yard. From the window of the hen house Charles watched them unhappily. They were all so merry and excited, and the pigs had come up to see Freddy off and were all talking at once and giving him a great deal more advice than he could possibly remember, and Hank, the old, white horse, was continually running back into the barn for another mouthful of oats, because he didn't know when he should get any good oats again, and Alice and Emma, the two white ducks, had waddled off down to the end of the pasture to take one last look at the old familiar duck pond, which they wouldn't see again until next spring. It made Charles very sad.

"Why don't you go out and say good-bye to them, Charles?" asked Henrietta. It made her feel bad to see him so unhappy, for she really had a kind heart, and way down inside of it she was very fond of him. But he was so careless and forgetful that she often had to be quite cross to him.

"No," said Charles mournfully. "No. I shall stay here. They've forgotten all about *me*. *They* don't care because I can't go with them. *They* don't remember who it was that gave them the idea in the first place. No, let them go. Heartless creatures! What do I care?"

"Nonsense!" said Henrietta. "Go along out." And so Charles ruffled up his feathers and held his head up in the air and marched out into the yard.

All the good-byes had been said and the travellers were ready to start. The barn-yard was silent as they formed in a line and marched out through the gate into the road that stretched away like a long, white ribbon to far distant Florida. First came Jinx, with his tail held straight up in the air like a drum-major's stick. Then came Freddy, the pig, and the dog, Robert, who was Jock's younger brother. After them marched Hank and Mrs. Wiggins, and the procession was brought up by the two white ducks, Alice and Emma, who were sisters. The mice—Eek, Quik, Eeny, and Cousin Augustus, ran along the side of the road so as not to be stepped on.

The stay-at-homes crowded out to the gate, waving paws and hoofs, and calling: "Good-bye! Good-bye! Don't forget to write! Have a good time and remember us to Florida!"

Overhead a flock of swallows darted and turned on swift wings. "Good-bye!" they twittered. "We'll see you in a week or two. We start south in about ten days ourselves."

Charles stood on the gate-post and watched the little procession march off down the road. Smaller and smaller it grew, and then it went over a hill, and the white road was empty again. But long after it had gone Charles sat on. And his tail feathers drooped, and his head dropped down on his chest, and a great tear splashed on the gate-post. But luckily no one saw him cry, for the animals had all gone back to their daily tasks.

At least that was what he thought. But Henrietta saw him from the window of the hen house.

IV

AND so the animals started out into the wide world. Although it was late in the fall and the branches were bare, the sun was bright and the air was fresh and warm. For some time they walked along together in silence, for they were a little sad at the thought of the comfortable home and the good friends they had left behind. But the smiling valley through which the road ran was too pleasant to be sad in for very long, and pretty soon Freddy, who was very clever, began to sing a song he had just made up. And this is the song he sang:

Oh, the sailor may sing of his tall, swift ships,
Of sailing the deep blue sea,
But the long, white road where adventures wait
Is the better life for me.

On the open road, when the sun goes down,
 Your home is wherever you are.
The sky is your roof and the earth is your bed
 And you hang your hat on a star.

You wash your face in the clear, cold dew,
 And you say good-night to the moon,
And the wind in the tree-tops sings you to sleep
 With a drowsy boughs-y tune.

Then it's hey! for the joy of a roving life,
 From Florida up to Nome,
For since I've no home in any one spot,
 Wherever I am is home.

There were a good many other verses—too many to put down, for Freddy made them up as he went along, and there was a chorus to each verse that went like this:

Oh, the winding road is long, is long,
 But never too long for me.
And we'll cheer each mile with a song, a song,
A song as we ramble along, along,
 So fearless and gay and free.

And pretty soon, as their spirits rose, and they thought of the adventures that lay ahead of them and the merry life they would lead, they all began to sing. They roared out the chorus with a will, and even the mice sang in their little, squeaky voices. The mice had got tired walking by this time, because their legs were so short, and so Mrs. Wiggins had invited them up on her back, which was so broad that there was no danger of their falling off, and they could sit there and enjoy the scenery and watch everything go by, just as you do from the window of a train.

All the morning they went steadily on. Every now and then they would have to go to one side of the road to let an automobile or a farm wagon pass them, and every time that happened the people would stare and stare. "Why, just look at those animals!" they would exclaim. "Did you ever see anything like that in your life?" And after they had gone by, the people would stop their automobiles or their horses and stare after them until they were out of sight.

About noon they climbed a steep hill, and from the top they could see ahead of them a broad valley, very much like the one through which they had come. And beyond the valley were more hills.

"This is all strange country to me now," said Hank, the old, white horse. "I've driven as far as this with Mr. Bean, but I've never been down into that valley. We'd better have a look at the map."

"There's a stream crossing the road half-way down the hill," said Robert, the dog. "Let's go down there."

So they went down and camped beside the stream, and the larger animals went in wading and splashed each other and laughed and shouted, and the two white ducks, Alice and Emma, swam about looking like two white powder-puffs, because that is what they like to do best. But Jinx, the cat, stayed on the bank and studied the map that the robin had drawn for him, to see if they were going in the right direction.

Then, when the animals were tired of splashing about in the stream, they came up on the bank and rested, and Jinx showed them the map. "We have to go across that valley and those hills, and then across another valley, and more hills, and then we come to a river," he said. "And we follow the

"We have to go across that valley and those hills."

river until we come to a village, and there we shall find a bridge."

"But will the people in the village let us cross the bridge?" asked Eek.

It was funny to see him and the three other mice sitting peaceably beside the cat, but Jinx had promised not to chase them, and they were not afraid. Cats very seldom make promises, but when they do, they always keep them. Their word is as good as their bond.

"I have heard Mrs. Bean say to Mr. Bean," Jinx answered, "never to cross a bridge until you come to it. So we'd better not worry about this one. And now don't you think we'd better be getting on?"

So they got up and started down the hill. Halfway down they had their first adventure.

They heard an automobile behind them and turned out to let it go by. It came along, rattling and bumping, for it was not a very good automobile, and as it passed them, a man with a big, black moustache leaned out and stared in surprise.

"Hey, sonny," he said to the boy who was driving, "wait a minute. Look at them animals. By gum, I never see anything like that before!"

The boy, who had a very dirty face, stopped the automobile, and they both stared back at the animals.

"There's nobody with 'em," said the boy. "Who do you suppose they belong to?"

"Dunno," said the man, and began to get out. "But we'll just drive 'em down to my place, I guess. If they do belong to somebody, we'll get a reward for 'em, and if they don't, we'll keep 'em ourselves. The cow looks like a good milker. Can't say much for the horse, though. Homely brute!"

Hank gave a loud snort at this, for while he was not a vain horse, he had a proper pride in a neat appearance, and he thought the man's remark insulting. Which indeed it was.

"That's a nice pig," said the boy. "We haven't had roast pig in a long time, pa."

"Nor roast duck," said the man, and he licked his black moustache and looked greedily at Alice and Emma. "I'll get a rope and tie the cow, and you take some stones and drive the dog away." He reached into the car for his rope.

This was too much for the animals, who had been undecided what to do.

"I don't care for these people *at all*," said Mrs.

Wiggins emphatically. "Robert, you and Jinx chase that dirty-faced boy away before he can pick up any stones. Don't hurt him; just give him a good scare. I'll attend to the man." And lowering her horns she galloped straight at him.

Now, cows are almost always good-natured and peaceful animals, and the man was very much surprised. He tried to dodge behind the car, but she scooped him up in her horns and tossed him high in the air. And as he went up, Mrs. Wiggins put her forehead to the back of the automobile and pushed it ahead so that it would be under him when he came down. Which he presently did, with a thump, on the automobile top. He bounced once or twice like a rubber ball; then, frightened but unhurt, peered over the edge of the top at Mrs. Wiggins, who was walking around the car and shaking her horns and mooing in a terribly frightening way. She was really laughing, but the man didn't know that.

Meanwhile the dog and cat had chased the boy away across a field. And he was even more badly frightened than the man; for after they stopped chasing him, he kept on running, and after he was out of sight, they could still hear his terrified yells.

31

"There! I guess we settled *them!*" said Mrs. Wiggins. And she sat down in the road and bellowed with laughter until the tears ran down her cheeks, and the man with the black moustache shivered with fear. Mrs. Wiggins was very fond of a joke.

Pretty soon the animals started on again, and when they had gone half a mile or so, they looked back and saw the man climb slowly down and get into the automobile. But he did not come after them: he turned round and went back up the hill, and went home another way.

Mrs. Wiggins was a character. That means that when she did anything, she always did it in a little different way than anyone else would have done. And she did a good many things that nobody else would ever have thought of. There were two spiders, Mr. and Mrs. Webb, that lived up in the roof of the cow barn. Of course they had heard everything that had gone on the night the animals had had their meeting, and the next morning Mrs. Webb slid down a long thread and landed on Mrs. Wiggins's nose. At first Mrs. Wiggins shook her head and asked the spider to get off; she tickled. But

Mrs. Webb crept up close to the cow's ear and said: "I want your advice about something."

This flattered Mrs. Wiggins, because very few people ever ask a cow's advice about anything. So she said she would listen. Now spiders have very little voices, and even animals, who hear better than people, have to be very close to them to understand what they say. So Mrs. Webb crept still closer to Mrs. Wiggins's ear, and said: "Mrs. Wiggins, me and Webb have been talking it over, and we'd like to go on this trip with all you animals. It's cold here in the winter, and there are very few flies, and we have to sleep most of the time. Do you suppose it could be managed?"

Mrs. Wiggins thought and thought, and finally she said: "I'd be glad to do you and Mr. Webb a good turn, because you keep the cow barn clear of flies in the summer. As far as your coming along goes, that isn't bothering me, for you can ride on my back. But I've been wondering how you could catch enough flies to keep you alive."

"That's just the difficulty," said the spider. "We'd be travelling all day, and even if we spun a web at night, when we camped, the flies wouldn't get caught in it till next morning, and then we'd be gone."

Mrs. Wiggins thought some more, and then she said: "I've got it! Suppose you spin a web between my horns! Then you'll have it with you all day, and you can catch plenty of flies." And Mrs. Webb was so delighted that she danced about on all her eight legs, and tickled Mrs. Wiggins's ear terribly, and then she ran up her thread as fast as she could and told her husband. And so they went along on the trip to Florida.

This was just the kind of thing Mrs. Wiggins was always doing.

The animals went on down the hill and across the second valley. They met a few people, in automobiles or on foot, but the people only stared and did not try to stop them. Then about four o'clock Alice and Emma, who had got tired and were riding on Hank's back, began quacking excitedly.

"There's something funny coming down the road after us in a cloud of dust!" they said.

"Automobile, probably," said Hank.

"It's too small for an automobile," said Alice.

"Then it's a man," said Mrs. Wiggins.

"It's too small for a man, and it comes too fast," said Emma.

Then they all stopped and looked, and away back on the road they saw a tiny cloud of dust coming along at a great rate, and they could not imagine what it could be. And then the wind blew the dust aside for a moment and they all set up a cheer. For they saw that it was Charles, the rooster, and Henrietta, his wife. And if you don't believe that a hen can run fast, you should have seen them coming down that road.

In a very few minutes they had caught up with their friends, and then there was a great shouting and laughing and asking of questions, but they were both so out of breath that they could not speak for quite ten minutes.

Henrietta spoke first. "Good gracious, what a day I've had!" she exclaimed, fanning herself with her wing. "Yes, we decided to come. Charles felt so bad this morning when you all started out. So I got my sisters to take his place in the mornings. There are eight of them, you see. That makes one for each day in the week, and one over, to look after the children, or help out if one of the others is sick."

"But can your sisters crow?" asked Freddy.

"Crow?" said Henrietta. "Of course they can crow! Any hen can crow if she wants to, better than any rooster that ever was hatched."

"Why don't they ever do it then?" asked Jinx.

"Good gracious, what a silly question, cat! The roosters would never get up at all in the morning if the hens started to crow. They'd loaf round and sleep all day. They do little enough as it is. But at least they're out of the hen house early in the morning so their wives can get some work done. H'm! Crow indeed! I guess not!"

The animals were all glad to have Charles and Henrietta with them, and they went on for a way, and camped that night under a big oak-tree by the road-side. For a time they sat about and told stories and jokes and made plans for the future, but they were all tired, and one by one they dropped off to sleep. Before Charles's eyes closed, he looked drowsily up at the starry sky above him, and at the long, mysterious, white road by which they had camped.

"What a wonderful time we're going to have," he muttered sleepily. "This is the first time since I was a chick that I haven't had to worry about getting up in the morning.

"Oh, the winding road is long, is long,
  But never too long for me.
And we'll cheer each mile . . . mile'th song . . .
    song. . . ."

His voice trailed off into silence, and he was **sound**
asleep.

V

AT the first glimmer of daylight next morning Charles awoke. He stretched his wings, flapped them a couple of times, and then, before he knew what he was doing, gave a loud crow.

He had perched on a limb of the oak-tree, and just under him Hank was standing, fast asleep. Horses can sleep standing up as well as lying down, because they have four legs and don't fall over, and Hank had gone to sleep that way because the grass was wet with dew, and he thought if he lay down in it, it would be bad for his rheumatism. When Charles crowed, Hank opened his eyes.

"Goodness!" he said. "You startled me! I thought you were not going to crow this morning. You said you were going to sleep till ten o'clock."

Charles looked foolish. "I suppose," he said, "that I've got so in the habit of getting up early and crowing that I do it without thinking."

"Well, in that case," said Hank, "I don't see why you complain so much about it. If you do it without thinking about it, it's just like breathing, and nobody ever complains about having to breathe."

"No," said Charles, "that's gospel truth!"

"I expect," said Hank, "that you've complained about it for so long that you do that without thinking, too."

This was a little hard for Charles to understand, but he thought about it for a while. And then he said: "You're right, Hank. I never realized it before. I don't really mind getting up and crowing a bit, now I come to really think of it. But," he added in a whisper, "don't tell Henrietta I said so."

By the time the sun was up the animals were all up too, and getting their breakfast. Hank and Mrs. Wiggins ate the long, juicy grass that grew beside the road, and Freddy ate the acorns that had fallen from the oak-tree, and Charles and Henrietta and the mice ate beechnuts from a beech-tree near by. Charles and Henrietta ate the nuts whole, but the mice held them in their forepaws and stripped off the husks with their sharp little teeth and ate the sweet kernels. And Mrs. Wiggins gave the dog and cat some milk, and the spiders sat up between Mrs. Wiggins's horns, where they had spun their web, and caught flies for breakfast.

They all breakfasted well but Alice and Emma. Ducks like to eat the juicy weeds and things that they find in the mud at the bottom of ponds, but of course there wasn't any pond handy, so Alice and Emma ate a few beechnuts that the mice shelled for them, and said that they would wait for the rest of their breakfast until they came to the river.

It was not until early in the afternoon that they came down a long hill into another valley and found the wide, swift river that the robin had marked on the map. Here they sat down and rested while the ducks dived for their meal in the shallow water under the bank.

Mrs. Wiggins was very much interested in the diving. "I do wish I could do that," she said. "Just think how exciting it must be to be down among the fishes and see all the queer things that grow on the bottom, and look up at the sky through the green water!" She had been leaning over the edge as she talked, and all of a sudden the bank gave way, and down she went into the water with a terrible splash, and there she was, sitting in the river with the water up to her neck.

The animals all rushed to help pull her out, but they could do nothing for her, for she was quite helpless with laughter. She laughed and laughed. "Here I am," she said, "down among the fishes where I wanted to be. Nothing like having your wishes come true."

But suddenly she stopped laughing. "Goodness me!" she exclaimed. "Where are Mr. and Mrs. Webb? They were sitting on my head when I fell in."

She clambered hurriedly up the bank, and then they all searched the bushes along the shore for a long distance down-stream. But the spiders were nowhere to be found.

"Well," said Mrs. Wiggins at last, "I guess they're gone. They won't drown—that's a comfort. They'll float down and land somewhere, but the current is pretty swift, and they may go miles before they can get ashore. I don't suppose we'll ever see them again. I hope this will be a lesson to me—cutting up silly didos on the bank like a two-weeks-old calf!" She was very angry with herself.

The animals all agreed, however, that it wasn't her fault, and pretty soon they started on again. They followed the river for some time, and by and by saw the white houses of the village and the high arches of the bridge ahead of them.

"I vote we wait till after dark to go through the village," said Robert. "Those people are sure to chase us or try to lock us up or something, if they see us."

This seemed a sensible plan, so they sat down by the river to wait. Pretty soon they heard a rattling and a puffing coming along the road, and then an automobile came into sight, and in it were the man with the black moustache and the boy with the dirty face. And behind it ran a black dog, twice as big as Robert and three times as fierce-looking.

As soon as the man saw the animals he stopped the machine. "Now we've got 'em, sonny," he said. "Here, Jack," he called to the dog. "Sick 'em, Jack! Go after 'em. Chew 'em up!"

The dog growled and bounded across the road, but Mrs. Wiggins lowered her horns and shook them threateningly, and Robert barked, and the cat arched his back and spat, and even Freddy squealed angrily. And the dog stopped.

"You'd better not bother us," said Mrs. Wiggins.

"I don't want to," said the dog. "I haven't got anything against you. But he'll beat me if I don't."

"What do you stay with him for if he beats you?" asked Robert.

"Where could I go if I didn't stay with him?" asked the dog.

"Come along with us," said Robert, and he told him where they were going.

"That's fine!" said the dog, and he walked toward them, wagging his tail.

"Hey, Jack!" called the man angrily. "What's the matter with you, you useless, good-for-nothing cur? I'll beat you within an inch of your life!" And he picked up a stick and started after the dog.

But now that Jack had found some new friends, he wasn't afraid of his cruel master any more. He turned with a growl, and before the man could lift the stick, he was flat on his back on the road with Jack's forepaws on his chest.

Then the man changed his tune. "Good Jack! Good old boy!" he said. Let me up, that's a good dog." But Jack did not move, and the other animals came and sat in a ring around the man, and the boy jumped out of the automobile and ran away across the fields yelling, just as he had done before. I don't know that I blame him.

After a while, when they thought they had scared the man enough, they let him up, and he walked over to the automobile without a word and got in it and drove off. Then Jack told them that he had lived with the man for five years, and that it had indeed been a terrible life, for the man hardly gave him anything to eat, and he beat him nearly every day.

"I guess Mr. Bean is a pretty good master after all," said Hank. "At least he never beats us, and if some things aren't just as we should like to have them, it's because he's poor and can't afford to have them better."

"You don't happen to have a bone about you, do you?" asked Robert. "I haven't had a good gnaw since I left home."

"The farm where I have been living is just a little way back along this road," said Jack, "and I buried two good bones in the orchard yesterday. If you'll come with me, we'll get them. Can you spare the time?"

"There's plenty of time," said Robert, "because

we can't start on until after dark." So the two dogs raced off together to get the bones.

All this time Mr. and Mrs. Webb had been floating peacefully down-stream on the swift current of the river. Spiders can float, because they are very light. But they can't move round much on the water, because it is so slippery under their feet, and for every step they take in one direction they slide two in another. So Mr. and Mrs. Webb just sat still and sailed along and admired the changing scenery of the banks.

"I don't know why anyone should want a private yacht when they can travel like this," said Mr. Webb. "It's delightful. Though I must say I am sorry to miss the trip to Florida."

"No use crying over spilt milk," said his wife. "Or spilt spiders either, and that's what we are. We'll never see *those* animals again. Even if we could get over to the bank and climb up to the road before they came along, they'd go right by without either seeing or hearing us."

"But," said Mr. Webb, "they spoke of crossing a bridge further down the river. If we got to that before they did, we could try to make them see us, anyway."

"Now, that's an idea," exclaimed his wife. "You've got a head on you, Webb. I always knew you did have, in spite of what my father said about you before we were married."

"I know what he said well enough without your repeating it every five minutes," grumbled Mr. Webb. "He said I didn't have gumption enough to catch a lame fly without wings. That's what you're thinking about, I suppose."

"No," said Mrs. Webb, "I was thinking about the time he said you'd never be hanged for your beauty, and you ought to——"

"That's enough," said Mr. Webb crossly. "You'd be better occupied thinking about what we're going to do when we get to the bridge than raking up all those old things. There it is just ahead of us."

So Mrs. Webb stopped talking, and they began to think up a plan, and by the time they were almost to the bridge, they had decided what they would do.

The current bore them swiftly down toward one of the arches, but under the arch some dead branches were sticking up through the water, and they caught hold of these and climbed up over them to the bridge.

"They haven't come by yet," said Mr. Webb, after they had examined all the footprints of animals that were plainly marked in the dust on the floor of the bridge. "There have been some horses and dogs along here to-day, but no cows or pigs or cats or ducks."

So they both climbed up to the iron beam on one side of the bridge, and each of them fastened the end of a thread to the beam, and then they dropped down, spinning out the thread as they went, and carried it across the bridge and fastened the other end to the iron beam on the other side. They did this several times, until they had a bridge of threads, strong enough to hold them both, right across the roadway and about ten feet above it. Then they walked out to the middle of it and waited.

Of course they did not know that the animals had decided to wait until after dark to cross the bridge, and by the time the sun had gone down and the stars had begun to wink out, and lights to twinkle in the houses, they commenced to be worried. But there was nothing to do but wait, and at last they heard the shuffle and patter of many paws and hoofs, and the animals came down the road and on to the bridge. They were walking as

"Here I am," she said, *"down among the fishes."*

quietly as possible, so that the people in the houses would not hear them, but spiders can see in the dark, and when Mrs. Wiggins's nose was just under them, they each slid spinning down a thread and landed on it.

Mrs. Wiggins gave a tremendous sneeze that nearly blew them off, for they had tickled her nose dreadfully, but they hung on tight.

"Dear me!" said Mrs. Wiggins. "I do hope I'm not getting a cold, being out so late in the night air!"

But Mr. Webb had crawled up close to her ear, and he said: "It's us, Mrs. Wiggins—the Webbs. We waited for you on the bridge."

Then Mrs. Wiggins told the other animals what had happened, and they were so glad that they gave a loud cheer, and they all said how happy they were to have the Webbs with them again, and how clever the spiders were to have thought of such a good scheme. And all the villagers came to their doors and looked out to see what the noise was, but by this time the travellers were across the bridge and didn't care.

That night they camped in a deserted barn, and it was lucky they did, for toward morning a heavy shower came up. But the roof was still good, and though most of them woke up when the rain started, they were dry and warm, and soon they went back to sleep again with the pleasantest sound in the world in their ears—the soft drumming of rain on shingles.

VI

SO for two weeks the animals travelled on toward Florida.

"It must be a long way," said Hank. "The weather doesn't seem to get any warmer."

"But it doesn't get any colder, either," said Mrs. Wiggins, "and down here the leaves are still on the trees. When we left home, the trees round the farm had all shed their leaves and were ready for the winter."

"Well, I don't care how far it is," said Hank. "We're certainly having a good time. I shall be almost sorry when we get there."

Nearly every day now large flocks of birds passed by them overhead, southward bound. And one morning the same swallow who had first put the idea of migrating into Charles's head dropped down from the sky and circled about over them. She had left home two days earlier, and she gave

51

them all the news of the farm, and messages from their relatives, and told them that Mr. and Mrs. Bean were well, but that they felt very bad that the animals had left them.

"At first," she said, "Mr. Bean thought someone had stolen you, but then somehow he guessed that you had decided to go to Florida for the winter. I heard him tell Mrs. Bean that he hoped you'd have a good time and come back safe and sound in the spring. And he said that he was going to try to make things more comfortable for you, although he didn't know how he'd manage it, because he didn't have money enough to fix things up the way they ought to be."

When the animals heard this, they felt a little sorry that they had left Mr. Bean without saying good-bye. "But we'll bring him something nice from Florida when we go back," they said.

So far they had kept away from the cities as much as possible, because they were afraid that the people would not understand that they were migrating, and would try to lock them up and keep them. And when they had to go through villages, they always waited till late at night, when everyone was asleep. But at last one day, away off in the distance, they saw a little speck of gold, that glittered and sparkled in the bright sunlight.

They wondered and wondered what the gold thing could be, but none of them knew, and pretty soon, as they went along, the road turned into a street, and there were houses on both sides of it and trolley tracks down the middle. And the speck of gold grew bigger and bigger. It looked as if a great golden balloon was tethered among the trees ahead of them.

"We're coming to a city," said Robert. "We'd better turn off this road and go round it."

"I wish I knew what the gold thing is," said Freddy, the pig. Freddy had a very inquiring mind.

Just then a little woolly, white dog with a very fancy blue ribbon around his neck came along, and Freddy asked him.

The little dog stuck his nose up in the air. "Don't speak to me, you common pig," he said.

"Eh?" said Freddy. "What's the matter with you? I only asked you a civil question."

"Go away, you vulgar creature," said the little dog snippily.

"Oho!" said Freddy. "You're too stuck up to

talk to a pig, are you?" And he laughed and ran
at the little dog and rolled him over and over in the
road till his white coat and blue ribbon were both
grey with dust. Then he stood him on his feet and
said: "Now answer my question."

Then the little dog meekly told him that the
thing that looked like a golden balloon was the
dome of the Capitol, and that the city they were
coming to was Washington, where the President
lives. And when Freddy had given him a lecture
on politeness and had helped him to brush the dust
off himself, he let him go.

"I'd like to see the President," said Hank.

All the others said they would too, but they were
afraid to go into the city because the people might
lock them up, and boys were sure to throw stones
at them.

But Jinx, the cat, said: "I vote we go, just the
same. I don't believe the President will let them
do anything to us. And we can see the Capitol
and the Washington Monument and maybe go up
to the White House and call on the President."

So they decided to go, and started down the
street toward the city. All the people came out
on their door-steps to watch them go by, but nobody

bothered them, and by and by they came to the
Capitol. They stood for a long time and admired
the big, white building, with its many columns and
its gilded dome, and then they walked round to the
side and admired it some more, and while they were
standing there, two senators in silk hats came out
and saw them.

"I didn't know animals ever visited the Capitol,"
said the first senator.

"Neither did I," said the second senator. "But
I don't see why they shouldn't. I think it's rather
nice."

Then a third senator came out and joined the
other two, and he said: "By George! I have heard
about these animals! They belong to one of my
constituents. They're going to Florida for the
winter, and I believe they're the first animals that
ever migrated. This, gentlemen, is one of the most
important occurrences in the annals of this august
assemblage. I'm going to order a band, and take
them round and show them the city."

So he went in and ordered the band, and told the
other senators, who put their heads out of the windows and smiled and waved to the animals.

"What's a constituent?" asked Mrs. Wiggins.

But none of the others could tell her, and to this day she has never found out.

Pretty soon the band came, and they struck up "Marching Through Georgia," and went up the wide avenue toward the White House, and the animals marched behind. First came the senator in his high hat, and then Charles and Henrietta, and then Mrs. Wiggins, with the mice sitting on her back, and then the two dogs and Freddy, the pig, and then Hank, with Alice and Emma on *his* back, and last came Jinx. They all walked in time to the music and held their heads up and pretended not to see any of the people that crowded the sidewalks, as everyone always does when he is in a parade. Beside them walked twenty policemen, to keep the people back and to prevent them from pulling the tail feathers out of the ducks or chickens to keep as souvenirs.

They went all over the city, and the senator showed them all the fine buildings and parks and monuments, and last they came to the White House. And there was the President out on the front porch, smiling and bowing to them, and as they filed past, he shook them each by a claw or a paw or a hoof. Even Eek and Quik and Eeny and

Cousin Augustus overcame their timidity and put their tiny paws into the President's big hand. They were all very proud.

And then they went on with the band playing a different tune every ten minutes, and the people cheering and waving handkerchiefs. When they got to the edge of the city, the band stopped and the senator made them a speech, which began:

"Friends and constituents, I am very sensible of the honour which you have done me to-day. To welcome a delegation of the home folks to the Nation's Capital is one of the few pleasures that cheer the burdened brow of those whose stern duty it is to keep their shoulder always to the wheel of the ship of State. And that reminds me of the story of the two Irishmen."

He told the story, and the animals laughed politely, although they did not see anything very funny about it, and that is why it is not written down here. Nor is the rest of the senator's speech written down, for the animals did not understand much of it, and I am not at all sure that the senator did either. But all agreed that it was a stirring speech.

Then the senator said good-bye to the adventurers, and the band played "Auld Lang Syne," and the animals went on their way.

"Well," said Mrs. Wiggins with a sigh, as she dropped off to sleep that night, "we certainly had a grand time. But I do wish I knew what a constituent is."

VII

ONE afternoon as the animals were marching along southward, they came to a deep, dark pine wood. It was a warm day, for they were getting near Florida now, and the road was very rough and stony. They were all hot and tired and cross. Even the good-natured Mrs. Wiggins grumbled as they plodded along between the rows of tall, gloomy trees.

"I wish these woods would come to an end," she said. "I never saw such a place! Nothing but pine needles—no grass, no water. And it's almost supper-time, too."

Robert put his nose up in the air and sniffed. "I smell rain," he said. And just as he said it, there came a long, low grumble of distant thunder.

"Well, we have got to find a shed or a barn or something," said Hank, the old, white horse. "I'm not going to stand under a tree in a thunder shower for anybody."

"My goodness!" said Henrietta crossly. "What's the good of *talking!* Why don't you *do* something? Jinx, why don't you climb a tree and see if you can see a barn?"

This was sensible advice, so Jinx climbed up to the top of the tallest pine he could find. When he came down, he said: "I saw the sun going down in the west, and I saw a thunder-storm coming up in the south. And the woods go on for miles and miles. But about half a mile farther along there is a little log house. And there is a chimney on the house, and there is smoke going into the chimney."

"Coming out of the chimney, you mean," said Hank.

"I mean just what I say," said Jinx. "There is smoke coming from all parts of the sky and gathering into a cloud and pouring down the chimney."

"Fiddlesticks!" exclaimed Henrietta. "I never heard of such nonsense!"

"I don't know whether it's nonsense or not," said the cat, "but that's what I saw. If you're so smart, why don't you climb up the tree and take a look yourself?"

Henrietta didn't dare climb the tree, so she said: "Fiddlesticks!" again in a very loud voice, and walked off.

It was getting darker and darker, and the thunder was rumbling and rolling and coming nearer and nearer.

"Well, there's no use quarrelling about it," said Mrs. Wiggins. "If there's a house, there's a barn, and if there's a barn, maybe we can get into it, out of the rain. I'm going along." And as this was a very sensible speech, they all started along after her.

Pretty soon they saw the log house. It sat back from the road, and was almost hidden by the trees and bushes that grew close up to its walls, so that if Jinx had not seen it from the tree-top, they might have walked right by and never noticed it. And sure enough, round the top of the chimney was whirling what looked like a cloud of smoke. It whirled round and round, and then plunged down, and as the animals had never seen smoke going the wrong way before, they just stood and stared at it.

"What did I tell you?" said Jinx.

But Henrietta didn't answer him; she went up close to the house and looked and looked; and although it was getting pretty dark, she saw that it wasn't smoke after all, but a flock of birds, who were coming from every direction and dropping down the chimney.

"There's your smoke!" she exclaimed scornfully. "Chimney-swallows! They live in the chimney, and they're going home to sleep. Smoke, indeed! That's the cat of it! Jumping at conclusions!"

"I'll jump at you if you say any more," said Jinx, "and pull all your tail feathers out."

"Come, come," said Mrs. Wiggins. "Stop your fighting, animals. If there are swallows in that chimney, it means that there hasn't been a fire built in the house in a long time. And *that* means that nobody lives there. Let's get inside."

Bang, bang-bingle BOOM! went the thunder. And the animals made a rush for the door and got inside just as the rain came down with a swish and a rattle.

There was only one room in the house, and in it were two chairs and a table and an empty barrel and a pile of old newspapers. Opposite the door was a big fire-place, and beside the fire-place was a neat pile of firewood. But everything was very

Bang, bang—bingle BOOM!

dusty. Nobody had lived in the house in a long time.

Outside, the rain was coming down in torrents, and the thunder and lightning were very bad indeed. But the animals were happy because they were dry. Only the mice, Eeek and Quik and Eeny and Cousin Augustus, were rather frightened, and at the first really sharp flash of lightning they dived down an old mouse hole by the fire-place and didn't come up until the storm was over.

After the thunder and lightning had gone farther away again, and the rain had settled down to a good, steady, all-night pour, Robert said: "It's getting cold. I wish Mr. Bean was here to build us a fire."

"There are some matches up here," said Charles, the rooster, who had perched on the mantel over the fire-place.

"I believe I could build one myself," said Robert. "I've seen him do it often enough. Chuck down a couple matches, Charles."

"And what about all those swallows in the chimney?" asked Henrietta. "I suppose you never thought about them!"

"We'll invite 'em to come down and sit around

the fire with us," said Robert. He called up to the swallows and invited them down, and pretty soon they began dropping down in twos and threes. They circled round the room, and then took their places in rows along the walls, for swallows don't perch as other birds do, holding on by their claws, —they hang themselves up by the little hooks they have on the tops of their wings. There were so many of them that the log walls were covered with them, and they looked like a beautiful, shining black tapestry.

Then Robert built the fire with newspapers and wood, and he held a match between his teeth and scratched it on the floor and dropped it on the papers. He singed his nose before he got through, but at last he got the papers to burning. Then all the animals had to squat down on the hearth and blow the fire to make it go, because he hadn't built it very well. But at last it burned up brightly, and then they all sat round and talked.

"I'd like to know who lived in this house," said Charles.

"Nobody knows," said the oldest swallow, who was hanging just over the door. And all the other swallows said: "That's so," and rustled their wings.

"Nobody lived here in my grandfather's time," said the oldest swallow.

"That's so," said the other swallows again.

"And nobody lived here in my great-grandfather's time."

"That's so."

"And nobody lived here in my great-great-grandfather's time."

"That's so."

"And nobody——"

"Excuse me," said Robert politely, "but I don't think you need go any farther back. Don't people ever come here at all?"

"Once in a while—" the swallow began slowly. Before he could go on, the youngest swallow piped up: "That's so."

The oldest swallow glared at him crossly, and his mother spanked him soundly for speaking out of turn. For it is a custom among the swallows for the oldest and wisest one to do all the talking, and for the others to say: "That's so" when he has finished. They do this because there are so many of them, and if they all talked at once in their little twittery voices, nobody would be able to understand what they were talking about.

"Once in a while," the oldest swallow went on, when the little swallow had been spanked and sent off to cry softly in a corner, "men come out to this house to look for the money that is supposed to be hidden here. It is said that a bag of twenty-dollar gold pieces is concealed in or somewhere near the house. But if that is so, nobody has ever found it."

The animals were all very much excited at this piece of news. Of course they could not use money themselves, but they thought how nice it would be if they could find the gold and take it back to Mr. Bean, who needed money so badly. Then he could buy all the things he wanted, and could repair the barn and the hen house, and perhaps put stoves in them to keep the animals warm in cold weather. So they all started hunting for the place where the money was hidden.

Hank tapped with his hoof on the floor and the walls, to see if they sounded hollow, and Jinx, the cat, climbed up on all the shelves and peered into cupboards, and Eek and Quik and Eeny and Cousin Augustus went back down the old mouse hole in the corner and scurried round under the floor and explored every crack and crevice. Even Mr. and Mrs. Webb slipped into the many cracks in some farm-house would wake up and bark sleepily as he heard them go by, laughing and singing and shouting to one another. They met very few animals or people on the road—only now and then a weasel or an owl, out hunting. And all the time they were getting nearer home.

VIII

EARLY the next morning Mr. Webb slipped out to get a breath of fresh air before breakfast. It was a bright clear morning. He took a long drink of fresh cold water from a raindrop, and then strolled along over the pine needles, humming to himself.

> *Oh, the winding road is long, is long,*
> *But never too long for me. . . .*

Pretty soon he met an ant.

"Good-morning," he said politely. "I am a stranger in these parts. I wonder if you can tell me if there is any good fly-catching in the vicinity?"

Now, almost always, if you speak to an ant, no matter how pleasantly, it will walk right by without answering. Ants do this because they are always busy, and they think conversation is a waste

69

of time. But Mr. Webb was a fine-looking spider, and the ant was rather flattered at being spoken to by him. So she said:

"I'm sure I don't know, sir. But there aren't many spiders in our neighbourhood, so I should think not."

"Ah, that's a pity," said Mr. Webb. "But it seems a very pleasant neighbourhood."

"We like it," said the ant. "Although it's not as pleasant as it used to be before the robber ants came. They live in an old stump down in the woods, and they are all the time stealing our children and robbing our storehouses."

"Dear me!" said Mr. Webb. "That is very trying."

"Indeed you may say so!" she replied. "It's hard enough to bring up a family of fifty children these days without having robbers about. We had to leave our old house and build a new one, deeper under the ground, so it wouldn't be so easy for them to break into it. Perhaps you'd like to see it?"

"I should be charmed," said the spider; and so she led him to where there was a little hole in the ground, out of which ants were carrying bits of dirt and sand, which they dropped outside before hurrying back for more. She led him down the hole and into a long tunnel. Part of the tunnel was so narrow that Mr. Webb had trouble squeezing through, but at last they came out in a large room which was really the ants' dining-room. Here there were dozen of ants running to and fro, popping in and out of doorways; some of them bringing food which they fed to the ant children, and others carrying out dirt from the tunnels and corridors they were building. They were all much too busy to pay any attention to their visitor, and they merely nodded and said: "How do," and went on with their work.

"It is a very pleasant house," said Mr. Webb, when he had been shown through all the many rooms and passages.

"Ah, you should see our other house!" said the ant with a sigh. "Gold floors in the reception hall and the dining-room, and a gold ceiling in the nursery! There wasn't a finer one in the woods."

Mr. Webb pricked up his ears. "I should think not!" he said. "Gold floors, eh? Now, may I ask how that happened?"

"Nobody knows," said the ant. "When my grandmother first moved into the house, some of them were there, and then later, when we enlarged the house and dug out more rooms, we found more of them."

"I should like to see that," said Mr. Webb.

"If I weren't so busy this morning, I would take you over and show them to you," said the ant.

"I am afraid I am keeping you from your work," said Mr. Webb; "so I'll just run along. But if you will show me where your old house is, I'll run in and look at it on my way back to join my friends."

So the ant went up to the door with him and showed him just which way to go, and then he thanked her politely for her hospitality and said good-bye.

Without much trouble he found the house that the ants had moved out of, and he crawled down the tunnel into the empty rooms that had once been a happy home, but were now empty and deserted. Soon he stood in the dining-room. It wasn't very large. Even Mr. Webb, who was a very small spider, could walk across it in five or six steps. But sure enough the floor was of bright, shining, yellow gold. And there were raised letters on it, and the figure of an eagle.

Now before he was married to Mrs. Webb, Mr. Webb had travelled round a good deal. And once he had lived in a bank. So he knew what a twenty-dollar gold piece looks like. And now he knew that the floor of this ants' dining-room was a twenty-dollar gold piece.

He did not wait to look at the other rooms, but hurried back to the log house as fast as he could go. For he remembered what the swallow had told them about the bag of gold, and he knew that he had found it.

This was what had happened. The ants who had first built that house had happened to begin digging just where the bag of gold was buried. It had been buried a long, long time, and the cloth had rotted away. The ants had tunnelled in and around the gold coins, and wherever one lay flat, they had made it the floor or ceiling of a room.

Mr. Webb got back just as the animals were ready to start. They gathered round him with their ears as close to him as they could get, so they could hear his tiny voice, and he told his story, and then they all rushed out to the ant house, and the two dogs and Freddy, the pig, started digging. Freddy dug with his long sharp nose, but the dogs dug with their forefeet. And in no time at all they had uncovered a great shining heap of gold coins.

Then they were all very glad, and Charles, the rooster, was so excited that he crowed and crowed.

But Henrietta said: "My goodness! Stop that noise! I don't see what you are all so happy about anyway. Now you've dug it up, what are you going to do with it?"

"Take it back to Mr. Bean, of course," said Robert.

"What are you going to do about going to Florida, then?" asked Henrietta. "Are you going to lug it all the way to Florida, and then back again? And what are you going to carry it in?"

"We hadn't thought about that," said the animals.

"Well, you'd better think about it now," said Henrietta. "The only thing you can do with the gold now is to bury it again, and get it when we come back from Florida. But I'm sure I don't know how we're ever going to take it to Mr. Bean."

"Oh, we can carry it in baskets or something," said Freddy. "Don't you worry about that, hen."

So they scraped the earth back into the hole and covered up the treasure, and then they started along.

IX

AS they went on southwest, the days grew hotter. Away back up north, at the other end of the road down which they were travelling, snow-flakes were flying, and Mr. Bean's breath was like smoke in the frosty air when Henrietta's sisters woke him in the morning and he put his head out of the window to see what the day was going to be like.

But down south the air was soft and warm, and the trees and the fields were green, and the animals tramped along merrily all day, and camped by the road-side at night. The only thing that worried them was how they were to get the gold coins back to Mr. Bean. There were about half a bushel of them, and even if they were in a sack or a basket, they would be much too heavy for one animal to carry, because gold is heavier than almost anything else in the world.

But Mrs. Wiggins, who always looked on the bright side of things, said: "We have got all winter in Florida to think about how to carry them. If we can't think of some scheme by spring, we aren't very bright animals. I for one don't intend to worry about it any more."

By this time the travellers had got used to being stared at by the people they met, and so almost always when they came to a village, they walked straight through it instead of going round. When they did this, Jack, the black dog, would go to the butcher shop and sit up on his hind legs and beg in the doorway, and usually the butcher would give him a piece of meat or a bone, which he shared with Robert.

A good many of the people had heard of them, too, and knew that they had come hundreds of miles down from the cold north to spend the winter in Florida, and these people would come out to meet them when they came to the edge of the town, and bring them things to eat, and make a great fuss over them. In one town a band came out to meet them, just as in Washington, and there were carriages for them, too, and all the animals but Hank and Mrs. Wiggins rode through the town in the carriages.

But, of course, there were bad people, too, who had heard about them, and thought it a good chance to get some fine animals without paying for them. One day, as they were going along by the bank of a muddy, sluggish river, two men with guns jumped out from behind some bushes. As soon as they saw the guns, the animals started to run, but they were not quick enough, and before they knew what had happened to them, Hank and Mrs. Wiggins had ropes around their necks and were being led off down the road.

The other animals knew that the men would shoot at them with the guns if they tried to help their friends; so they hid in the bushes, and then followed along, keeping out of sight.

Pretty soon the men came to a gate, and they led the cow and the horse through the gate and past a small, white house, and locked them up in a big, red barn. Then they walked back to the house, whistling, with their guns over their shoulders, to get their supper, for it was six o'clock.

"I guess there's *two* animals that won't do any more migratin'," said one.

And the other laughed a loud, coarse laugh and said: "They'll do a little work now, instead of loafing round the country."

And they opened the door and went into the house without wiping their muddy boots on the door-mat.

As soon as they had gone in, Jinx, the cat, sneaked up to the barn through the long grass. He crept along so very carefully that the tops of the grass hardly moved. He climbed up and looked in through the little, dusty window, and saw Hank and Mrs. Wiggins standing on the barn floor. Their heads drooped, and they looked very miserable and unhappy. Then he tapped cautiously on the window with his claw, and called in a low voice: "Hey! Hank!"

The horse jumped and raised his head. "Is that you, Jinx?" he said.

"Yes," said the cat. "I came to see if you were all right. The others are hiding in the bushes down by the river. We're going to try to rescue you."

"Well, I don't see how you're going to do it," said Hank. "We are both tied up, and the barn-door is locked. It's very discouraging, to come all this distance and get almost to Florida, and then be stolen. I'm sure I don't know what **Mr. Bean** will say."

"Now don't talk like that," said Jinx. "You'll escape somehow. We won't desert you. Do you suppose you could kick a couple of boards out of the side of the barn if you could get loose?"

"I won't say I couldn't," said Hank. "I've got my heavy shoes on. But it would take some time, and before I had made an opening big enough to get out of, the men would hear the racket and come out and tie me up again."

"We'll attend to that," said Jinx. "You just have patience, now, and I'll send the mice in to get you loose. They'll gnaw those ropes and straps off you in no time. Then I'll come and tell you when it's time to break out."

So Jinx went and told the mice, and they got into the barn through a crack in the floor, and gnawed at the ropes with their little, sharp teeth until they had cut them in two.

By this time it was dark, and Jinx and Freddy, the pig, and Charles and Henrietta and the two dogs and Alice and Emma came up to the house and peeked in the window. The two men had cleared off the supper table and were playing parchesi. They played four games, and between times they laughed and talked about how smart they were to have got two good animals without paying for them, and wondered how much money they would get for them when they sold them.

The big man was a very poor player, and he lost every game. He would study and study over his moves, but he always made them wrong. Now Freddy was a very good parchesi player, and it was all the other animals could do to keep him still when he saw the big man starting to make a wrong move. He would jump up and down in his excitement and mutter under his breath: "Oh, what a stupid move! Oh, what a stupid move!" And at last, when the big man had made a specially bad move and lost the fifth game, Freddy could stand it no longer, and he shouted out: "Oh, you big silly! Why didn't you move your *other man?* Now he's beat you again."

The men jumped up so quickly that they knocked over the parchesi board and spilled the men all over the floor.

"What was that?" said the big man.

"It sounded like a pig," said the other. "Up and after him!"

And they rushed out without even stopping to get their hats. But they grabbed up their guns as they went through the doorway.

The animals ran in all directions, but it was bright enough outside so that the men could see Freddy as he dashed out through the gate and down the road, and so they dashed after him. Now, Freddy was a very clever pig, but he wasn't much of a runner, and the smack, smack, smack of heavy boots on the hard road sounded louder and louder behind him, as the men caught up.

"They're going to catch me," he thought. "Oh dear! I do hope they don't like pork! The great stupid creatures! I could beat them at parchesi, and I could beat them at eating, and I'm ever so much brighter than they are. But they're going to catch me. And I've got more legs than they have, too!"

He didn't dare turn off the road because his legs were so short that he knew he would very quickly get tangled up in the bushes, but the road was close to the river at this place, and just as the big man reached out to grab him by the tail, Freddy dodged and jumped with a splash into the water. Most pigs don't like water any too well, but Freddy had been taught swimming by Emma, the duck, and he could do all sorts of fancy strokes, and could even swim on his back, which is something hardly any pigs ever learn to do. So he struck out bravely for the other shore.

The men stopped short, and the big one raised his gun to shoot. But the other said: "No, no! Don't shoot! We want to capture him alive and sell him." And he pulled off his coat and shoes and jumped in after Freddy.

The big man waited a minute; then he too laid down his gun and took off his coat and shoes and jumped in.

Freddy heard them puffing and blowing behind him like sea-lions, but he put his snout down into the water and swam the Australian crawl, the way Emma had showed him, and pretty soon he came to the other bank. There was no use climbing out and trying to run away, because the men would catch him; so he turned around and swam back again.

For quite a long time the men chased him, up and down and across the river, and once or twice they nearly had him, but he was very wet and slippery, so that there was nothing for them to get hold of, and every time he got away. And then at last he heard a dog bark.

The sound came from the place on the bank where the men had left their guns, and Freddy swam toward it. And there, close down by the edge of the water, were all the animals, and Hank and Mrs. Wiggins were there too, because they had broken out of the barn while the men were chasing Freddy.

Robert and Jack helped the exhausted Freddy out of the water, but when the two men started to follow him, they growled and barked and showed their teeth. Then the men swam down-stream a way, but the dogs followed along the bank and growled at them every time they tried to land. And at last they swam across the river and went home another way.

It was not a very pleasant way, because there was no road on the other side of the river, and to walk across fields in your stocking-feet is very painful. The sticks and stones hurt like anything. And they were wet through, and had lost their guns, and when they got down opposite their house, they had to jump in and swim across the river again. And then they found the horse and the cow gone, and a big hole in the side of their barn.

And when they got in the house, they were angrier still, for there was the parchesi board on the floor, and the parchesi men had rolled off into corners and under the stove and behind things. If the floor had been clean, it wouldn't have been so bad, but it was terribly dirty because they never wiped their boots on the mat when they came in, and so it was almost impossible to find the men. Indeed, there were three that they never did find. And so they could never play parchesi any more at all.

X

NOW as they went along, the weather got warmer and warmer, and so they got up very early in the mornings and did most of their travelling while it was still cool. About eleven o'clock they would stop under the shade of a big tree by the road-side, and lie about in the grass and talk until late in the afternoon. And then they would go on for a while until they found a good camping-place. When they came to a river or a pond, they would all go in swimming. It was the pleasantest life you can imagine.

One day, about noon, they were all sitting in the shade beside the road at the top of a steep hill. On the other side of the road was a house, but nobody was in sight but a little girl, who was wheeling her dolls up and down in a doll baby carriage.

Most of the animals were asleep, because Jinx, the cat, had been talking, and nobody paid any attention when he talked. That didn't make any difference to Jinx, though. He went right on telling how smart he was and bragging about what he could do.

That was the worst of Jinx: he always talked about himself. If the animals talked about automobiles, he told how much *he* knew about them, and how well *he* could run one; and if they said: "Let's go in swimming," he told what a fine swimmer *he* was, although they all knew he hated the water and couldn't swim two strokes.

To-day he was talking about bicycles.

"'Tisn't anything to ride a bicycle," he said. "I've ridden 'em—all kinds—bicycles and tricycles and velocipedes and——"

"Oh, you're a wonder!" said Freddy crossly, and all the other animals who were awake said: "Oh, *please* keep still, Jinx."

Alice and Emma, the two white ducks, didn't say anything, however, because they were always very polite, and were afraid of hurting Jinx's feelings. They were almost too polite, if such a thing is possible. But they were just as tired of hearing Jinx talk as the others were; so Alice said: "Come on, Emma; let's go play with the little girl." And they got up and ruffled out their feathers and waddled sedately across the road and up the path to the house.

The little girl was delighted to have someone to play with, and she put the ducks in the carriage with the two dolls and pretended that they were the neighbour's children, and that she had to look after them while their mother was out shopping. And she pretended that they might catch cold and wrapped them up in a little blanket, and Alice and Emma were so polite that they let her do it, although it was so hot that they nearly boiled.

Then the little girl said: "Are you comfortable, darlings?"

And Emma said: "Quack, quack!"

"Oh!" said the little girl. "She can say: 'Mamma!'" And Emma had to keep on quacking for quite a long time while the little girl hopped up and down and clapped her hands.

By and by the little girl got tired of this and said she would take them for a ride, so she wheeled them down the path and out into the road. Then she saw a bright blue butterfly and ran off across the field after it, leaving the dolls' baby carriage standing in the road at the top of the hill, near where the animals were resting.

Jinx was still talking about bicycles.

"I can ride backwards, and with both paws off the handle bars, and I can ride up and down stairs——"

"Oh, stop talking such foolishness!" said Henrietta. "You couldn't ride a bicycle. Your legs aren't long enough to reach the pedals."

"They wouldn't have to be," said Jinx. "I could do all that going down hill. Just start at the top, and *whizzz!*—down you go at sixty miles an hour! And——"

"Oh, stop *talking!*" exclaimed Henrietta. "I never heard such an animal! Brag, brag, brag! That's all there is to you! You wouldn't dare ride down that hill in that doll carriage there!"

"Ho!" said Jinx. "That's nothing! That's so easy it isn't worth bothering about."

"All right," said Henrietta. "Let's see you do it, then."

"I suppose you think I can't?" said Jinx.

"I think you won't," said Henrietta bluntly.

Jinx got up and walked over to the doll carriage

and climbed into it beside Alice and Emma and the two dolls.

"Why, it isn't anything," he said. "It isn't anything at *all!* Just slide down that hill? Pooh!" But he didn't seem very anxious to start.

"Please get out of the carriage, Jinx," said Emma. "There isn't room for all of us in here."

"Are you really going to slide down the hill, Jinx?" asked Alice. "Because if you are, I'm going to get out."

"Slide down that hill?" said Jinx. "And climb all the way back up again in the hot sun, just to prove I can do it? Huh! I should say not! If they don't believe me—well, they needn't, that's all!"

All the animals had waked up by now and had come out into the road.

"You don't dare slide down the hill," they shouted. " 'Fraid cat! Coward!" And Freddy made up a verse and sang it while he danced around the carriage on his hind legs.

> " 'Fraid cat Jinx,
> His tail's full of kinks!
>   He doesn't dare slide down the hill!
> See how he shrinks!"

Now Jinx had no intention of sliding down the hill, which was a good mile long, with a curve at the bottom, and he was thinking hard for some good excuse. But while he was hesitating, Freddy bumped against the wheel of the carriage and gave it just enough of a push to start it slowly down the hill.

"Hey! What are you doing?" yelled Jinx, too frightened to jump.

The animals stopped shouting and stood with their mouths open as the doll carriage gathered speed and shot away from them down the steep hill. They heard the scared quacking of Alice and Emma, and saw their little white heads peering fearfully out; they saw Jinx holding on for dear life with all his twenty claws as the carriage jumped and bounded from side to side of the road. And then it grew smaller and smaller and disappeared round the curve.

The animals were very much frightened, and they started down the hill as fast as they could go. Half-way down they heard a great noise behind them, and it was the little girl, who was coming after them, crying and sobbing at the loss of her dolls.

A very wet Jinx was crawling up onto the bank.

"That bad cat!" she wailed. "That bad, wicked cat! He stole my doll carriage and ran off with my dollies!"

The animals waited until she caught up, and Hank knelt down and let her climb up on his back. Then they went on.

Pretty soon they got to the curve at the foot of the hill. They went round it, and there was a bridge crossing a wide stream, and half-way across the bridge lay the doll carriage, upside down, and a very wet Jinx, with a bruise over one eye, was crawling up on to the bank out of the water. And out in the middle of the stream Alice and Emma were swimming about and quacking as if nothing had happened.

When the carriage had turned over, it had been going so fast that the ducks and the dolls and the cat had been thrown way up over the top of the bridge into the water. The dolls had sunk, and the cat had sunk, too, for a few minutes and had had a hard time getting ashore, for he wasn't much of a swimmer in spite of his bragging. But Alice and Emma hadn't minded a bit.

As soon as Jinx saw his friends, he tried to look as if he had done it on purpose.

"There!" he said. "I guess you won't dare *me* to do anything again! I guess I did it, didn't I? I guess *you* haven't got much to say!"

But the little girl jumped down from Hank's back and went over to him and began slapping him good and hard.

"You bad cat!" she cried. "You bad, *bad* cat! Where are my dollies?"

Jinx made himself as small as possible and put his head down between his paws and let her spank him. It didn't hurt as much as she thought it did, and as he said afterwards to Freddy—"it knocked all the water out of my fur."

But Alice and Emma dived for the dolls and brought them up and laid them on the bank to dry. And after a while, when the little girl was tired of spanking Jinx, she put them into the carriage again and Mrs. Wiggins pushed it back up the hill for her. But the little girl rode up on Hank's back.

After that, Jinx didn't talk so much. And if he did begin to boast, all the animals had to do was to say: "Kidnapper! Doll-stealer! Who got spanked by a girl?" And he would curl up and pretend to go to sleep.

XI

AND now at last one day when the animals had been walking all morning through wild and swampy woods, they came out at the top of a long slope that went down to a wide valley in which were many green trees and comfortable-looking, white houses. A soft wind blew over the valley, and puffed into their faces a sweet delicious perfume, that none of them had ever smelt before. They sniffed the air delightedly.

"Mmmmmm!" said Mrs. Wiggins. "Isn't that good? It's better than clover. I wonder what it is."

"I know," said Jack. "I've smelt it at weddings. See all those little green trees down there? They're orange-trees, and that smell is orange-blossoms."

"Look! Look!" squealed Freddy. "There's a palm-tree!"

"It's Florida!" shouted Jinx.

And all the animals shouted together: "Florida!" so that they could be heard for miles, and Alice and Emma hopped about and quacked and flapped their wings, and Charles crowed, and the dogs barked, and Mrs. Wiggins mooed, and Hank, the old, white horse, danced round like a young colt until his legs got all tangled up and he fell down and everybody laughed. Even the spiders raced round and round the web they had spun between Mrs. Wiggins's horns, and the mice capered and pranced.

"So this is Florida!" said Mrs. Wiggins. "Well, well!"

Then they started down the slope into Florida. And as they went, Freddy made up a song:

The weather grew torrider and torrider,
And the orange-blossoms smelt horrider and
*   horrider,*
As we marched down into Florida.

"But the orange-blossoms *don't* smell horrid," said Robert.

"I know it," said Freddy. "But there isn't any other word that rhymes."

"Well, make up another song, then," said Robert.

So Freddy sang:

Oh, the winding road to Florida
    Is a dusty road, and long,
But we animals gay have cheered the way
    With many a merry song.
Our hearts were bold—but our homes were cold.
    And that is why we've come
To Florida, to Florida,
    From our far-off northern home.

In Florida, in Florida,
    Where the orange-blossom blows,
Where the alligator sings so sweet,
    And the sweet-potato grows;
Oh, that is the place where I would be,
    And that is where I am—
In Florida, in Florida,
    As happy as a clam.

They all liked this song much better, and as they went along they sang lustily. They were so glad to have reached Florida at last that they forgot all about stopping to rest at noon, and they marched on until nearly three o'clock. Then Mrs. Wiggins sank down under a tree beside the road.

"I can't go another step!" she said. "I'm in a dripping perspiration. Charles, I'd take it kindly if you'd fan me with your wing for a few minutes."

So they all sat down and Charles very kindly fanned Mrs. Wiggins until she had cooled off. And as they were all pretty tired and hot, they decided to camp there that night and think about what they were going to do in Florida. And then in the morning they could go and begin doing it.

So they camped under the orange-trees and discussed all the things they could do, and at last they decided to go to the sea-shore, as Freddy said he understood the sea-bathing was very fine there.

"But how can we find the sea-shore?" asked Robert. "You ought to have had that robin draw it on the map."

Freddy said it would be easy to find because Florida was a peninsula.

"What's a peninsula?" asked Jack, and Henrietta said: "Oh, don't ask him! He's just trying to show off."

But Freddy said: "A peninsula is a piece of land

that is almost surrounded by water. That means that if you walk far enough in any direction but one, you will come to the ocean."

"Yes," said Robert, "but how do we know which direction is the one we ought *not* to walk in?"

"Why, the direction we came from, stupid," said Freddy. And he drew a little map on the ground and showed the animals what he meant.

So the next morning they started out to find the ocean. They travelled for four days before they saw it, away off in the distance, glittering and sparkling in the sunlight, and it was still another day before they came down to a broad beach of yellow sand and saw the great sheet of water stretching away before them for miles and miles. They just stood and looked at it for a long time, for none of them had ever seen anything like it before. And they rushed down the beach and swam out into the water.

So for a month they lived by the side of the ocean and rested from their long journey. They found an old barn not very far from the shore, and they cleaned it up and all lived there together happily. Every day at four o'clock they went in for a dip in the surf, and then they would lie round on the sand

and talk until supper-time. It was a very lazy and pleasant life that they lived in Florida.

But after a while they got tired of doing nothing and began to long for new adventures. "Besides, we ought to travel round and see the country," said Charles. "When we get home, and everybody asks us what Florida is like, we want to be able to tell them."

So they said good-bye to the sea-shore, and to the horseshoe crabs and jelly-fish, who had made things so pleasant for them during their stay, and set out for a tour of the state.

XII

DURING the next two months they visited all the principal points of interest in Florida, and saw all there was to see. They visited Palm Beach and the Everglades and Miami and the Big Cypress Swamp. And it was on the way across a corner of the swamp that they had a very exciting adventure.

It happened this way. When they first came to the swamp, most of the animals were afraid and did not want to go into it at all, for it stretched for miles and miles, and there were no roads or paths, and there was no firm ground to walk on, only water and mud and the great twisted, gnarly cypress roots. It was dark, too, because the trees grew so thick.

But Jinx said: "Oh, come on! Let's see what it's like. We don't have to go very far in. What are you afraid of?"

And so they started in.

At first it wasn't very hard walking, but soon the mud and water got deeper and the trees thicker together. And after a while longer there wasn't anything to walk on at all—only water and trees.

"I'm going back," said Mrs. Wiggins. And the other animals said they were too. Even Jinx agreed they couldn't go any farther.

But when they started to go back, they found that they hadn't the slightest idea which way to go. They had turned and twisted in and out among the trees so many times that they didn't know from which direction they had come. The water covered their footprints so they couldn't follow them. And over their heads the branches were so thick that they couldn't see the sun.

"Now we *are* in a mess!" said Henrietta, who had been riding on Hank's back. "I hope you're satisfied, Jinx!"

"It won't help any to call names," said Mrs. Wiggins. "Come along, let's try this direction. One way is as good as another, and this looks as if it might be right."

And so they went on, with Mrs. Wiggins in the lead. It was very dark and dismal. The water was black, and long beards of grey moss hung down from the branches of the trees. Again and again they had to swim, and the animals who could not swim climbed on the larger animals' backs.

At last it did seem as if they were coming out on dry land. Ahead of them they could see sunlight through the tree trunks, and they floundered and stumbled onward as fast as they could go. In a few minutes they came out on the bank of what seemed to be a small canal, and beyond the canal was a grassy meadow, green and pleasant in the bright sun.

"Well, this certainly isn't the way we came," said Mrs. Wiggins. "But, my word! that grass looks good! I guess we could get away with a few mouthfuls of that, eh, Hank? Come along, animals, let's swim over. It's something to stand on, at any rate."

"Look out! Don't bump your noses on those logs," said Jinx, pointing with one claw to what looked like a lot of tree trunks, lying half under water in the middle of the canal.

So they all swam over. But as they were climbing out on the farther bank, Henrietta began to cackle excitedly. "Look! Look! The logs are all coming to life!"

And sure enough, what they had thought were logs had suddenly started swimming after them. They were alligators!

"I certainly do *not* like this place!" said Mrs. Wiggins. But like most cows, she had a stout heart, and she turned round and lowered her horns and shook them threateningly at the alligators. "Keep away, now!" she said. "We won't stand any nonsense!"

But the alligators only laughed, and one of them said: "Oho! You won't, eh? Well, what did you come into our country for, then?"

"We're peaceable animals," said Mrs. Wiggins, "and all we ask is to be shown the shortest way out of your country. We are lost, and we shall be very much obliged to you if you will help us find ourselves again. But if you won't help us, we shall have to go on and find our own way out."

Then all the alligators laughed so hard that two of them choked, and their friends had to whack them on the backs with their tails. And they said: "Do you know where you are? You are on an island in the middle of the alligator country. You can't get away. And to-night we alligators are going to have you for supper."

The animals saw now that they were indeed in a bad fix. "This is even worse than being fricasseed," said Charles.

But Freddy, the clever pig, had an idea. And although he was very much scared, he said to the alligators: "Gentlemen, you will make a very great mistake if you eat us. We are not ordinary animals. We are the first animals in the world who ever migrated. We have come from far in the north; thousands of miles we have travelled, to visit your beautiful country, and to take back word of its loveliness to our people. Surely you would not be so inhospitable as to eat us for supper."

"He speaks very nicely," said one of the alligators, "but I am sure he would taste even better. He is so round and plump!"

But another one said: "There may be something in what you say, pig. We will take you to the Grandfather of All the Alligators, and you may tell him what you have told us. And perhaps he will let you go. And perhaps he will eat you for supper just the same. But that is for him to decide."

And so he led them across the island to where the water and the swamp began again on the other side. And he stood on the bank and called: "Oh, Grandfather of All the Alligators, there be strangers here who would have speech with thee."

Nothing happened for some time, and then there was a bubbling and a boiling of the water, and a huge head, as big as a barrel, appeared, and after the head a body as long as Mrs. Wiggins and Hank and Jack and Robert and Freddy together. It was the Grandfather of All the Alligators, and he was so old that there was green moss growing all over him.

He opened one wise old eye, and his deep grumbling voice said sleepily: "What do they want?"

"They don't want to be eaten for supper," said the other alligator.

"Eat them for lunch, then," said the Grandfather of All the Alligators, and began to sink out of sight again.

But Freddy rushed down to the edge of the water and shouted: "Oh, Grandfather of All the Alligators, we are strangers in your beautiful country and we have come thousands of miles to visit you and tell you of our own land, of which you have never heard."

The Grandfather of All the Alligators opened both eyes and stopped sinking.

"Why didn't you say so in the first place?" he asked. "That alters the case entirely. I hear very little news of the great world in this quiet spot. By all means tell me of your home."

"Oh, Grandfather of All the—" Freddy began.

But the Grandfather of All the Alligators stopped him. "It will be better," he said, "if you call me simply grandfather." And he closed his eyes and sank till everything but his ears was under water, and prepared to listen.

Then Freddy told of the life they had lived up north on Mr. Bean's farm, and of how cold it was in winter, and of their trip to the South. Every time he stopped for breath, the alligators, who were sitting around him in a circle, would say: "Yes, yes; go on!" And Freddy went on until he was tired, and then Jinx took up the story until *he* was tired, and then Charles went on with it. And by the time Charles had finished, and they had told everything they could think of, it was almost sunset.

Then the Grandfather of All the Alligators came

up to the top of the water again and opened his eyes and said: "I thank you for telling us of your wonderful country. It has been very interesting. And now, as it is almost supper-time, we will go on with the feast. I am sure you will all taste very much better for the entertainment you have given us."

At this the animals were very much alarmed. "You don't mean to say you meant to eat us all the time!" they cried.

"Why, of course," said the Grandfather of All the Alligators. "Nothing was ever said about our *not* eating you, was there?"

This made the animals very angry, and Jinx was so mad that he almost had a fit. "You mean to say," he screamed, "that you've gone and let us talk ourselves hoarse for nothing, you great big, muddy, long-nosed, leather-skinned hippopotamus, you? You ought to be ashamed of yourself! What do you suppose all the animals up north are going to think of you when they hear about it? Eating up visitors who come to make you a friendly call! A nice opinion they'll get of Florida!"

"My goodness, I should say so!" exclaimed Mrs. Wiggins. "And the President of the United

States, too. He shook hands with us and wished us a pleasant journey. What'll *he* say?"

"He'll send his army down here and drive all you alligators into the ocean; that's what he'll do!" said Jinx.

The Grandfather of All the Alligators smiled, and his smile was eight feet broad. "What you say may be so," he remarked. *"But*—who's going to tell him? Answer me that. Who's going to tell him? You, madam?" he asked Mrs. Wiggins. "No-o-o, I think not. You'll be eaten up, horns, hoofs and tail. And so——"

But Henrietta interrupted. *"We're* going to tell him," she said. "My husband and I. You may eat the animals, but you can't eat us, because you can't catch us. *We* can fly."

"My dear," said the Grandfather of All the Alligators, "I am more than eight hundred years old. I was centuries old when Ponce de Leon came to Florida to look for the Fountain of Youth. I remember Balboa well—a tall man with a black beard and a shiny steel hat. He made the same mistake you did, my friends—he mistook me for a log. But he was more fortunate than you. He got away with merely the loss of one of his boots." The Grand-

107

father of All the Alligators smiled at the memory. "A delicious boot that was, too—old Spanish leather. I chewed on it for half a day.

"Yes, as I was saying, I am very old. Yet in all my eight hundred years I have never seen or heard of a hen or a rooster who could fly like other birds."

Now it is true that hens and roosters cannot fly as well as most birds, but they don't like to be reminded of it. Henrietta became very angry.

"Is that so!" she exclaimed. "Well, if you've kept your eyes shut for eight hundred years, it's no wonder you don't know anything! Never saw a rooster who could fly, eh? Well, you're going to see one now. Charles," she said to her husband, "fly up in those trees on the other side of the water."

Now the trees were quite a long way off, and Charles had never in his life flown farther than from the ground to the top of a fence. "Good gracious, Henrietta," he whispered, "I can't fly up there. I won't be able to go half that distance, and I'll drop into the water and the alligators will eat me."

"They'll certainly eat you if you *don't* fly up there," she whispered back. "You've *got* to do it. It's our one chance of escaping. If they think you will go back and tell the President, they will let us go."

"Well, I'll try it," said Charles. So he kissed Henrietta good-bye and squared his shoulders and flapped his wings and started, while all the animals cheered, and the alligators giggled and poked each other in the ribs with their elbows.

Charles flew up into the air—up, up, higher than he had ever been before, as high as the tops of the trees. And then he started across the water.

Down below, the animals held their breath as they watched him. They saw him flapping his wings so hard that feathers flew out of them and floated downward. But he could not get any higher; he was coming slowly down toward the water, and two of the alligators plunged in and swam out to be under him when he came down.

"He'll never make it," said Mrs. Wiggins sadly. "Never in the world!"

But suddenly they saw him stop moving his wings. He spread them out and held them motionless, and then, to the amazement of all the onlookers, he went straight across the water—faster, faster, and landed with a flutter in the trees.

What had happened was this. There was a

strong wind blowing across the swamp, but the island, shut in by walls of high trees, was like a room, and the wind did not come down there at all. It was this wind that had caught Charles and blown him safely across, but of course none of the onlookers knew this, and they thought that he had done it himself.

Then all the animals set up a great cheer, and the alligators had nothing to say at all, and the Grandfather of All the Alligators opened his eyes wider than he had opened them in six hundred years and exclaimed: "Well, upon my word! I never should have believed it! Never!"

But Henrietta said: "*Now* what are you going to do about eating us?"

"Why, that was all a joke, my dear," said the Grandfather of All the Alligators. "We alligators will have our little joke, you know. Do tell your accomplished husband to come back, so that we can thank him for this fine exhibition, and then he will show you the way out of the swamp, and part in peace and goodwill."

"Oh yes, you old fraud!" said Henrietta. "Ask him to come back so you can eat him? No, Charles will stay right where he is, in the top of that tree."

"We alligators will have our little joke, you know."

"Your suspicions are most unjust," said the Grandfather of All the Alligators with a sigh. "We wouldn't harm him for worlds. We respect and admire him greatly. However, I see you are anxious to be gone, and it is indeed getting late. My children," he said to the other alligators, "show these animals safely to the edge of the swamp, and see that no harm comes to them. Good-bye, my friends. I thank you one and all for your entertainment. I am sorry that you took our little joke in earnest. However, that is past now. No hard feelings, I trust?"

"Oh, none at all!" said Henrietta sarcastically. And the Grandfather of All the Alligators sank slowly out of sight.

The alligators showed the animals a dry and easy path to the edge of the swamp, and they were very happy when they were on dry land once more. Charles had not come down within reach of the alligators, but had fluttered along in the tree-tops. Then the alligators said good-bye and wished them a pleasant journey.

When the animals had gone on a little way, they looked back and saw the alligators sitting in a row and looking after them, and great tears were roll·

XIII

NOW after the adventure with the alligators the animals rested for two days, and then they went on seeing the sights of Florida. They made a great many pleasant friends among the natives, and even Mr. and Mrs. Webb made the acquaintance of a number of very interesting and agreeable spiders, with whom they discussed fly-catching, and compared notes on weaving and other matters of interest.

But at last one morning when they awoke, the sky was full of flocks of birds—bluebirds and blackbirds and red-wings and yellow-hammers and purple grackles—all flying steadily northward. And then they knew that spring had come and it was time for them to be starting back home.

"Well, I for one shall be glad to get back," said Mrs. Wiggins. "We've had a grand time travelling, but home's a pretty good place. The snow is all gone by this time, I expect, and Mr. Bean is getting ready to plant his potatoes and corn and cabbages."

"And the old elm by the barn is all covered with buds," said Charles.

"And the ice is gone out of the duck pond," said Alice and Emma.

"And Mr. Bean will need me to help with the spring ploughing," said Hank.

"Come along, animals," said Freddy. "Let's start." And so they said good-bye to Florida and started home.

They had been travelling for about a week when they came one morning to a big field which was all heaped with tin cans and old shoes and ashes and rubbish of all kinds. There were prickly thistles growing in the field, and a goat was eating them.

"Good-morning, goat," said Freddy.

"Good-morning, pig," said the goat. "Have a thistle? They're delicious."

"No, thanks," said Freddy.

"Have you ever eaten one?" asked the goat.

"No," said Freddy. "They never looked very good to me."

"You'd be surprised," said the goat, "how tasty they are. Just take a nip of this big one here."

Freddy didn't want to try the thistle, but he was always very polite and didn't like to hurt the goat's feelings, so he took a large bite.

As soon as he had taken the bite, he wished he hadn't. The prickles tickled his mouth horribly and stuck into his tongue, and he coughed and sneezed and squealed and grunted and ran round and round in circles, while the other animals laughed and the goat looked at him in surprise. And at last he got it out of his mouth.

"I'm very sorry," said the goat. "Perhaps there was something the matter with that one. Now *here's* a nice one. Or perhaps you'd rather have a bit of old boot. There were two fine ones left here yesterday. I've eaten one, but——"

"No, thank you," said Freddy firmly. "Some people say a pig will eat anything, but really—— One must draw the line somewhere, and I draw it at old boots."

"Well, well," said the goat with a sigh, "there's no accounting for tastes. I hoped that I might persuade you animals to settle down and live here with me. But of course if you don't like thistles, or boots——"

"We don't," said Mrs. Wiggins. "Any of us."

"Then that settles it," said the goat sorrowfully. "Because there's really nothing else here. I like it. But it's very lonesome. No one to talk to all day but the stupid cart-horses who bring the rubbish here to be dumped. And I do like good conversation."

He was so lonely that the animals spent the rest of the day with him and told him of their travels. Just as they were leaving, late in the afternoon, a farm wagon came along, piled high with rubbish. It belonged to a man who was moving into another house, and he had brought all the stuff that he didn't want to keep. He was going to throw it on the dump heap. On the very top of the load was a funny old-fashioned carriage.

The man threw the rubbish out of the wagon, carriage and all, and drove away.

"Must be some boots in that lot," said the goat, licking his lips, and began poking round in the heap.

But Jinx and Freddy had walked over and were looking at the funny old-fashioned carriage. They talked together in undertones for a few minutes,

116

and then Jinx said: "Hey, Hank! Come here. Do you suppose you could draw this carriage?"

"Draw *that?*" said Hank indignantly. "I've drawn heavier wagons than that many's the time.

"Oh, I know you can draw it," said Jinx. "What I mean is—can you draw it the way it is, without any harness and straps and things?"

"No," said Hank. "I'd have to have a collar and traces and bridle and bit and surcingle and——"

"Oh, we don't know what any of those things are," said Jinx, "and anyway we haven't got them. But here's an old piece of rope. Suppose we could tie that to the handles of the carriage and put it over your shoulders. Could you draw it then?"

"Why, I won't say I couldn't," said Hank. "But what do you want the carriage for anyway?"

"If you can draw it," said Jinx, "we can put the gold that we found in the ants' house in it and take it back to Mr. Bean."

Hank thought this was a fine plan, so Freddy got the rope and Jinx tied it to the handles of the carriage. All cats are good at tying knots. The stupidest cat can tie forty knots in a ball of yarn in two minutes—and if you don't believe it, ask your grandmother. So this was easy for Jinx. And then they looped the rope over Hank's shoulders and he pulled the carriage up on to the road.

The carriage had two seats and the top was like a square umbrella, with fringe around the edges. It was called a phaeton, and if you think that is a funny name, all I can say is that it was a very funny carriage. The animals laughed like anything when they saw Hank pulling it out of the dump heap, and Mrs. Wiggins laughed so hard that she had to lie down right in the middle of all the old tin cans.

But when Freddy told them what they could use it for, and how they could carry the gold back to Mr. Bean in it, they were very much pleased. The two dogs gathered together a number of things that they thought Mr. Bean would like and put them in the carriage. There was an old straw hat and an old overcoat, and two pails, one half full of red paint and one half full of green paint. "He can use them to paint the house," said Robert. And there was also a plaid shawl for Mrs. Bean. These were all things that people had thrown away on the dump heap, but the animals thought Mr. Bean could use them. And if he didn't use them, he could throw them away and nobody's feelings would be hurt

Then they said good-bye to the goat. He didn't feel so bad about their going now, because he had a fresh wagon-load of rubbish to look over, and had already found a lot more old boots to chew on. Then all the small animals climbed into the phaeton and they started off. Robert and Emma and Jack sat on the front seat, and Freddy and Alice and Jinx and Henrietta sat on the back seat. The four mice played tag all over the carriage for a while, and then they curled up in the bottom and went to sleep. And Charles perched on top of the square umbrella.

When they had gone a little way, they looked back and waved good-bye to the goat, and he waved back at them. They could see him chewing away contentedly, and the ends of two old shoe-strings were hanging out of his mouth.

XIV

UPHILL and downhill the phaeton rolled along northward. Sometimes Mrs. Wiggins drew it and sometimes the two dogs drew it, but whenever they went through a town, or were where they were meeting a good many people, Hank drew it, because then the people didn't stare so. Once, when they went through quite a large town, Hank wasn't feeling very well, so Mrs. Wiggins put the rope over her shoulders and drew it for him. But the people all rushed to their doors and crowded round them and laughed so to see a cow harnessed to a carriage that Mrs. Wiggins got quite angry.

"I'm not going to have anybody laughing himself into a fit on *my* account," she said. And after that she would draw it only when they were on very lonely roads.

They were all so anxious to get home again that

they travelled faster than they had on the way down, and it was not many days before they saw in the distance the white house and the red barn where Hank and Mrs. Wiggins had been taken prisoner by the two men with guns. And there were the two men standing by the gate and talking.

The animals stopped and looked at one another, and at first they didn't know what to do. Some of them thought they ought to wait until after dark and then sneak by when the men were asleep, but the others were in a hurry, and as the men didn't have their guns, they decided to disguise themselves and try to get past.

So Jinx got out the two pails of paint they had put in the carriage, and with a stick he painted Hank with red stripes up and down, and Robert with green stripes lengthwise, and Mrs. Wiggins he dotted all over with large red and green polka dots. He wanted to put some stripes on her horns, too, but she wouldn't let him on account of Mr. and Mrs. Webb.

Then Jack, the black dog, got up and sat on the front seat of the carriage, and he had on the straw hat and the overcoat, so that from a little way off he looked like a very small man. And Freddy sat

Mrs. Wiggins he dotted all over.

on the back seat with the shawl over his head. Jinx painted circles around his eyes so that he looked as if he had spectacles on. His own mother wouldn't have known him.

All the small animals got into the carriage and hid under the seats. Mrs. Wiggins walked behind and Robert ran along underneath, and they went on toward where the men were. When the men caught sight of them, they opened their mouths wide and just stared. The big man had a pipe in his mouth and it fell out on to the road and broke, but he didn't even notice it. He just went on staring. Neither of the men had ever seen such queer-looking animals before.

"What is it?" said the big man at last, looking at Hank. "A zebra?"

"Maybe it's part of a travelling circus," said the little man. "I never see a horse with red stripes before."

"Who's the old lady in the back seat?" asked the big man. "She don't live around here, does she?"

"Never saw her before," said the other. "Why don't you ask the coloured coachman?"

But before the big man could get up his nerve to call out to Jack, who did indeed look like a coloured

coachman in his straw hat and overcoat, the carriage
went past him and he caught sight of Mrs. Wiggins.

"Great earth and seas!" be exclaimed, and both
he and his friend jumped clean over the gate and
crouched down behind it, shivering with fear.

"It's a leopard," said the big man. "Look at the
spots! A leopard with horns!"

"Leopard nothing!" said the little man. "It's a
cow. Look at the shape of it!"

"I never saw a cow all covered with red and green
polka dots," said the big man. "It's a leopard."

"It's a cow," said his friend. "Maybe it's got
some queer kind of measles."

"If it had the measles as bad as that, it would be
sick in bed," said the other. "It's a leopard."

"Maybe it's got walking measles," said the little
man. "I've heard of that kind. But it certainly is
a cow."

"It's not!" shouted the big man. "It's a leopard!"

"It's a cow," repeated the little man angrily.

"It's a leopard!"

"It's a cow!"

"A leopard!"

"A cow!"

The little man was so enraged that he suddenly

slapped the big man hard on the cheek, and the last the animals saw of them, the big man was chasing his friend across a field. "A cow, eh?" he was roaring angrily. "Don't you dare say that word again!" And they grew smaller and smaller and disappeared in the distance.

As soon as the animals had gone three or four miles farther they stopped and all went in swimming in the river that ran beside the road, to see if they could get the paint off. But it wouldn't come off, no matter how hard they scrubbed. Jinx sat on the bank and laughed and laughed.

"You'll laugh out of the other side of your mouth, young man, if *I* catch you," said Mrs. Wiggins. "You knew it wouldn't come off all the time."

"It'll come off if you rub hard enough," said Jinx.

"Yes, and so will my skin," snapped Mrs. Wiggins.

"Anyway," said Jinx, *"you* can't catch me. Who's afraid of an old cow? Who——" But Robert had sneaked out of the water and come up behind Jinx, and just then he grabbed him by the neck. "I can catch you, though," he said. "Freddy, get the pail of red paint. We'll just fix Jinx up

125

so he'll look as funny as the rest of us. Then we'll have something to laugh at too."

So Freddy brought the pail of red paint, and Robert held Jinx over it and started to dip him down. He only intended to dip him in a little, so that he would have a bright red tail, but Jinx began to wriggle and twist so that Robert lost his hold, and splash! down went Jinx into the paint.

He jumped out at once and ran around like a crazy thing, rolling on the ground and scraping against trees, but the paint stuck to his thick fur and he couldn't get it off. For the paint wasn't very deep in the pail and he hadn't gone all the way in, so that the front part of him was black and the back part was red, and he was probably the funniest-looking cat that anybody ever saw.

From this time on the animals attracted a great deal more attention on the road than they ever had before, and if the people had stared at them when they were just regular animals, they stared twice as much now that they were all striped and spotted with red and green.

Some of the people were scared too. There was a tramp lying asleep one day by the road-side, and just as the animals were passing him, Alice sneezed.

A duck doesn't sneeze very loud, but tramps don't sleep very soundly, and this tramp was wide awake in an instant. He stared at the animals, and then he looked up at the sky and down at the ground and back at the animals again, and then he pinched himself hard two or three times. And then, finding that he was really awake, he gave one more horrified look and with a dreadful yell turned and ran. He ran so fast his feet hardly seemed to touch the ground. They saw him go up one hill and disappear over the top, and then in a few minutes they saw him, very much smaller, going up another hill way beyond. And he was running just as fast as when he started. For all I know he may be running yet. I don't know that I blame him.

But the animals did not like to be stared at, and they did not like to scare people, so they did most of their travelling at night. They would sleep all day, and then along about sunset they would wake up and have a little something to eat and start out. They had some beautiful moonlight nights about this time, so that it was easier and pleasanter travelling by night than by day. The moon was like a great golden lantern hung in the sky to light them on their way, and now and then a watch-dog

XV

AT last, late one night, they came down into the deep, dark pine woods where they had discovered the empty log house, and where they had found the bag of gold. Although the moon was shining brightly, it was very gloomy in the woods, and they were walking slowly and not talking very much, because they were thinking how they were going to carry the gold back in the carriage, and how glad Mr. Bean would be when he saw it. They had almost reached the log house when Robert and Jack both stopped at exactly the same moment and began sniffing the air.

"I smell tobacco," said Jack. "Not very good tobacco."

"It comes from the direction of the house," said Robert. "Somebody's smoking."

"All honest people are abed by this time of night," said Mrs. Wiggins. "Whoever it is is up to no good. Hank, you and I had better stay here, and the other animals can sneak up to the house and see what those people are up to."

So Freddy and Robert and Jack and Jinx went very quietly up to the house. As soon as they got near it, they saw that there was a light in the window.

"I don't like this," said Jinx. "I hope they haven't found our gold."

"I wish the swallows were awake," said Freddy. "We could ask them about it. But let's look in the window."

So they sneaked up and looked in the window, and there were three men sitting round the table and smoking clay-pipes. They were very rough-looking men, and they wore caps pulled down over their eyes, and they all had revolvers and dark lanterns, so the animals knew at once that they were burglars. On the table was a big heap of everything you can imagine—gold watches and pocket-books and money and silver forks and spoons and ear-rings and bracelets and diamond rings. They were all the things that the burglars had stolen from the farmers who lived near the pine woods.

The biggest of the three burglars was dividing

the heap of things into three parts. "One for you, and one for you, and one for me. One for you, and one for you, and one for me." But he wasn't dividing them very fairly. For each time he said: "One for you," he would pick up a small thing that wasn't worth very much, like a small spoon or a ten-cent piece, and put it in front of one of his companions. But when he said: "One for me," he would take out a gold watch or a ten-dollar bill or a jewelled bracelet all set with diamonds and put it in front of himself.

But the other burglars were very much smaller men and so they didn't dare say anything, although they looked very much discontented with their shares.

Now the window through which the animals were looking was rather high up, as windows go, and although the two dogs and Freddy, the pig, could see in by putting their forepaws on the window-sill and stretching their necks, Jinx was too short, and he had to climb up and hang on by his claws. He didn't mind this particularly, because his claws were sharp and strong, and he could have hung on like that for hours. But there was a big brown moth who was also trying to look in the window at what

131

the burglars were doing, and it kept fluttering round on the pane right in front of Jinx's nose, so that half the time he couldn't see a thing.

At first he spoke to it politely, and asked it if it wouldn't please move up a little higher, where it could see just as well and wouldn't be in his way.

"Move up yourself!" growled the moth. "I was here first."

"Of course you were," said Jinx patiently. "But you must realize that I can't move up. And I should think common politeness——"

"Oh, shut *up!*" said the moth.

So Jinx didn't say any more, but he made up his mind to give that moth a lesson. So he let go for a mniute with one forepaw, and made one slap at the moth and scooped it right off the window.

But Robert, who was standing next to Jinx, was doing something that all dogs and a good many people do. When anything surprised or interested him very much, he opened his eyes very wide, and when his eyes opened, his mouth seemed to come open too. So he was standing with his mouth wide open staring at the burglars, and when Jinx hit the big brown moth with his paw, he knocked it straight down Robert's throat.

"Arrrrrrgh!" said Robert. "Woof!"

"What's that!" said all the burglars at once, and they jumped up and bent over the table to blow out the lamp. But as they all bent over at exactly the same time, their three heads came together in the middle, crack! And then the light was out and the animals couldn't see anything more, but they could hear the burglars rubbing their bumped heads and groaning.

For quite a long while the animals waited for something to happen, but nothing did. The burglars were evidently badly scared. They seemed to be whispering together, and at last Jinx said: "I'm going in to see what they're doing. I noticed when we came up to the house that the door was open a little way, and I think I can get in."

So he went round to the door, and sure enough it was open a crack, and he made himself narrow, as cats can, and slipped in. It was so dark inside that the burglars could not see anything at all, but Jinx could see them quite plainly. Cats can see in the dark. He jumped up on the mantelpiece to be out of the way, and sat down.

The two small burglars, whose names were Ed and Bill, were in a corner, trying to open one of

the dark lanterns, so they could light it. But as
they never used the lanterns, but only carried them
to show that they were burglars, they didn't know
how to open it. The big burglar, whose name was
Percy, was standing by the table, on which were the
three piles of stolen things that he had been dividing up, and he was feeling with his fingers in the
other piles and taking out the biggest things and
putting them on his own pile. But he couldn't see
what he was doing, and pretty soon he knocked a
watch and an emerald necklace off on the floor.

At the sound Ed and Bill started up. "What
you doin' over there, Percy?" Bill whispered
hoarsely.

And Ed said: "He's after them jools."

"Oh, I am *not!*" said Percy. "I was just feeling
for the matches."

"Oh, you was, was you?" said Ed. "Well, you
just come over here and give us a hand with this
lantern."

So Percy hastily stuffed a handful of ten-dollar
bills into his pocket and came over to them.

"Why don't you light the lamp?" he asked.
"We're perfectly safe. That noise wasn't anything."

"Maybe so," said Bill. "But I'm going to have a look round with the lantern first. Here, see if you can get it open."

They were all standing close to the fire-place, and as Percy took the lantern, Jinx, who never could resist a joke, reached out and dug his claws into his shoulder.

"Ouch!" yelled Percy, dropping the lantern with a crash. "What d'ye mean, sticking pins in me like that?" And he struck out with his fist in the darkness and hit Bill on the nose.

Bill had just been going to say: "I didn't touch you, silly!" but when that hard fist hit him, he changed his mind and flew at Percy, and in a second they were rolling on the floor and clawing and kicking and pulling each other's hair like wildcats.

They rolled toward the table, and Ed, who was afraid that they would knock it over and spill all the money and jewelery on the floor, took a match from his pocket and scratched it on the mantelpiece just under where Jinx was sitting, doubled up with laughter at the commotion he had caused. The match flamed up, and by its light Ed saw Jinx.

Now, if you are a rather timid burglar, and you light a match in a dark room and see a cat that is half black and half red—for Jinx had been dipped in the paint pot, you remember—if you see such a cat grinning at you within an inch of your nose, you will probably do just as Ed did. He dropped his match and let out an awful yell.

When he yelled, Bill and Percy stopped fighting and sat up. "What's the matter?" they asked.

"There's a red and black cat sitting on the mantelpiece and grinning at me!" said Ed in a scared voice.

"Fiddlesticks!" said Percy, and Bill said: "Nonsense!" and then he too lit a match. He was near the window as he did so, and there was Freddy, the pig, with his nose against the glass, staring in for all he was worth to see what was going on inside.

Then it was Bill's turn to drop his match and yell. "A pig with spectacles on is looking at us through the window!" For, of course, Freddy still had the circles around his eyes that Jinx had painted there.

"Fiddlesticks!" said Percy again, but he didn't say it quite as loud. And Bill and Ed didn't say anything.

There was silence for a few minutes, while the three scared burglars tried to get up enough courage to light another match. Then through the silence came the faint sound of wheels on the road outside.

"Listen!" whispered Percy. "Somebody coming. I'm going out to have a look. It won't be black and red cats, and pigs with glasses on, anyway." And he slipped silently out of the door.

The other two burglars tiptoed to the door and peered out after him, but although it was bright moonlight outside, the trees were so thick round the house that they could not see the road. And then, as they waited, came a terrible yell, and it was three times as loud as Ed's yell and Bill's yell put together. And they heard footsteps running, and Percy dashed up to the door, his eyes nearly starting out of his head with fright.

"Run! Run for your lives!" he panted. "Out on the road there's a tiger harnessed to a carriage and behind the carriage there's a leopard with horns, as big as a cow. Run, or we shall all be eaten up!" And he dashed off into the woods and the two others rushed out of the door after him, and the animals could hear the crash of branches and the thump of heavy feet die away in the distance. And

I may say here that they never saw either Ed or Bill or Percy again.

Of course what had happened was this. Mrs. Wiggins and Hank had got tired of waiting, and when they had heard the first two yells they had started down the road to see what was going on. They had not seen Percy come out of the door, and when he saw them and let out his terrible yell, they had been much more scared than he was. Indeed, Mrs. Wiggins was quite faint and had to lie down for a few minutes by the road-side while Charles and Henrietta fanned her with their wings.

"I'm all of a flutter!" she said. "Oh my, oh my! Just put your hoof on my side and feel how my heart beats, Hank. What a dreadful experience!"

But pretty soon she was able to get up and be helped into the house.

The burglars had left all the things they had stolen behind them in their flight, but as the animals had no matches, and as it was late, they decided not to do anything about them until morning. So they all curled up comfortably on the floor and went to sleep.

XVI

ALICE did not sleep very well that night. She had a stomach-ache. And she had a stomach-ache because she had eaten two chocolates and a caramel and a horehound drop that Robert had given her out of a bag of candy that he had found by the road-side. Robert had offered Emma some too, but she had very sensibly refused it. Candy doesn't agree with ducks.

So, as she couldn't sleep, no matter how hard she tried, Alice got up before daylight and went out into the woods. The cool morning air made her feel sleepy, so she thought she would try again, and, having found a sheltered spot under a big pine, she tucked her head under her wing and dozed off. When she woke up, the sun was shining and the swallows were pouring like smoke out of the chimney in search of their breakfast.

Alice called to one of them and asked him about the burglars.

"They've been here about a month," said the swallow. "They go out every night and rob the farmers' houses, and then come back and sleep all day. They usually get back about this time every morning, so you animals had better look out."

"I don't think they will be back *this* morning," said Alice. "But tell me, did they dig up the gold we found when we were here before?"

"No," said the swallow. "They haven't touched it."

"Thank you," said Alice. "That was all I wanted to know. Good-morning." And she hurried back to tell the others that their treasure was safe.

But when she got back to the house, she stopped in amazement on the threshold. Her sister, Emma, was waddling importantly up and down with a bracelet set with big blue sapphires round her neck and a beautiful bag, all made of little links of pure gold, tucked under her wing. The four mice, with diamond rings round their necks like collars, were playing tag in a corner, and they sparkled and glittered like little streaks of fire as they chased one another. Henrietta looked very queenly with a hoop of rubies set on her head like a crown. She was bending down and trying to see herself in the little mirror set in the cover of a powder box, which she had snapped open with her claw. But Mrs. Wiggins was most gorgeous of all. There was a rope of pearls about her big neck, and a platinum wrist watch on her left ankle. She had hung an emerald necklace on each horn, and they hung down and bobbed and dangled beside her broad, pleasant face like enormous ear-rings. And she had powdered her wide, black nose until it was as white as flour. She looked truly reckless.

Alice, after a moment's astonishment, entered into the fun. She found a thin, gold chain with a diamond and pearl locket which she hung round her neck, and then she went over to where Henrietta was still admiring herself in the powder-box cover, and asked if she might have some powder for her bill.

"There isn't any left," said Henrietta.

"I'm sorry, Alice," said Mrs. Wiggins. "I'm afraid I used it all up. There's so much of me to powder, you know. I do wish I could see myself. Though I must say I don't believe I have improved my appearance much. I must look like an over-dressed washerwoman. You can't do much with a cow," she added sadly.

Then Robert and Jack played a game. Each took six bracelets, and Mrs. Wiggins stood perfectly still, and they tried to throw them over her horns. But they weren't very good at it, and after Mrs. Wiggins had been hit on her nose several times, she said she guessed she wouldn't play any more, as they were knocking all the powder off.

Then Henrietta said: "What are we going to do with all this jewellery?"

"We ought to give it back to the people it was stolen from," said Hank.

"All very fine," said Henrietta. "But how do you propose to do that?"

Hank said he didn't exactly know. So they talked it over for a while and at last hit upon a plan. And after breakfast they loaded all the stolen things into the carriage and started out for the nearest farm-house.

When they got there, there was nobody in sight, but Jack and Robert barked until at last a woman came to the door to see what was the matter. She was a large, fat woman, and looked quite a lot like

Mrs. Wiggins. She was wiping soap-suds off her hands on her apron, because she had been washing her husband's other shirt.

"Land sakes alive!" she exclaimed when she saw the animals all grouped about the carriage. "What is this, a circus?"

It took quite a long time for the dogs to make her understand what they wanted her to do. They ran back and forth between her and the carriage, and at last she followed them. When she saw the heap of money and jewellery she gave a loud cry and seized the hoop of rubies that Henrietta had worn on her head.

"Land of love!" she cried. "Here's the ring that Cousin Eunice gave me last Christmas, the one the burglars stole when they broke into our house a month ago. And here's the emerald necklace I won as a prize at the pedro club last winter. And here's Hiram's gold cigarette case."

She ran to the corner of the house. "Hiram! Hiram!" she called. "Come here this minute."

So pretty soon Hiram, her husband, came from where he had been resting, up in the hay loft. And he found twenty dollars, beside the cigarette case, that the burglars had taken from him.

"Now, how do you suppose these animals got these things?" he said. "Do you suppose they found the place where the burglars hid them?"

"I don't know about that," said his wife. "But I do know that they brought them here so we could pick out what belonged to us. Such good, clever animals! I'm going to kiss every one of you!" Which she did, even the mice, who were scared to death. She looked very funny after she had kissed Mrs. Wiggins, because a lot of the powder came off on her face.

"Now," she said, "I'm going to go over to Aunt Etta's with these animals, because I saw her gold soup tureen among those things." And she climbed in the phaeton and they started off, while Hiram went back to do some more resting in the hay loft.

Aunt Etta was an educated woman. Every evening she sat on the porch and read the newspaper until it got so dark she couldn't see, and then she went in and lighted the lamp and finished reading it.

So when she had taken her soup tureen and one or two other things that the burglars had stolen, she said: "I know who these animals are. I saw a piece in the paper about them only last week. They're migrating. They came from way up north and went to Florida for the winter. They're very clever animals indeed. I expect they're on their way home now, as it's spring."

"Well," said her niece, "they won't get home until fall at this rate. They'll have to visit about a hundred farms to get all this stuff back to the people it belongs to. It's too bad they can't find a quicker way."

"A lot of the things have been advertised for in the paper," said Aunt Etta. "How would it be if we put an advertisement in, saying that all the things were here and the people could come here and get them? Then the animals wouldn't have to traipse all over the country, and they could go on home in a day or two."

The niece thought this was a good idea, and the animals looked at one another and nodded, and so Robert barked very loud to show that they thought it a good idea too. Then Aunt Etta got up. "I'll go in and telephone the newspaper office right away," she said, "and have the advertisement put in to-night. And then we'll give these animals something to eat and a place to be comfortable. They must be tired, having come such a long way."

So she telephoned the newspaper office, and then she went out in the barn and got some oats for Hank, and she showed Alice and Emma where the duck pond was, and introduced them to her own ducks, and she found two bones for the dogs, and a piece of cheese for the mice, and a saucer of cream for Jinx, and she cooked up some corn-meal mush for Charles and Henrietta, and led Mrs. Wiggins out into the pasture, where there was a very superior quality of grass. If she had noticed Mr. and Mrs. Webb she would probably have tried to catch some flies for them, she was such a kind and generous old lady, and so grateful for the return of her gold soup tureen.

Then, when the animals had all been given the things they liked best to eat, she sat down on the porch and told her niece everything she had read in the paper for the last six weeks.

XVII

SO for two days the animals stayed at Aunt Etta's, who, as Mrs. Wiggins said, was kindness itself. They sat on the front porch with her while she read the paper, and they ate the good things she prepared for them. A good many of the animals in the neighbourhood who had heard about them came to call and to ask about their travels, and as there were so many who were interested in their adventures, Charles very kindly consented to give a lecture in the big barn on the second evening. The name of the lecture was *A Trip to the Sunny South,* and it was a great success.

Then on the third day all the farmers and their wives from far and near who had had things stolen by the burglars gathered in Aunt Etta's parlour, because that was the day the advertisement in the paper had told them to come, to get their things back. All the jewellery and money and watches and silverware were tastefully arranged on little tables covered with white doilies, and all the farmers had to do was to pick out the things that belonged to them. And when they had all got their property back, they made a great fuss over the animals, and one nice old lady, whose name was Mrs. Trigg, and who owned the rope of pearls that Mrs. Wiggins had dressed up in, said: "I wish there was something we could do for these good, kind animals to show them how much we appreciate what they have done for us. Can anyone think of anything?"

The farmers and their wives all clapped their hands and cheered at this, and made more of a fuss over the animals than ever, but no one could think of any way to reward them.

Then Robert had an idea, and he went up to Mrs. Trigg and barked three times.

"I believe that dog understood what you said," said Aunt Etta. "Just see the way he's looking at you."

Then Robert ran a little way toward the kitchen, and stopped and looked back; so Aunt Etta and Mrs. Trigg followed him, and he went straight to a shelf in the kitchen and stood on his hind legs and put his forepaws on the edge of it and looked over his shoulder at them and barked again.

There were a number of things on the shelf. There was a photograph of Aunt Etta, and a photograph of her married daughter who lived in Rochester, and a spool of black darning-cotton, and an alarm-clock, and a butcher's bill, and a picture postcard of Niagara Falls, and seven beans, and a box of matches, and quite a lot of dust. The dust was there because Aunt Etta, although she was a kind-hearted woman, wasn't a very good house-keeper. She spent too much time reading the news-paper.

"Now, what do you suppose he wants up there?" said Mrs. Trigg.

"Why I do believe," said Aunt Etta, and I think she blushed a little—"I do believe he wants that picture of me!" And she took the picture down and gave it to Robert.

Of course the picture wasn't what Robert wanted at all but he was too polite to let her know it, and he thanked her by wagging his tail and smiling the way dogs do. And then he put his forepaws on the shelf and barked again.

"He wants something else, too," said Mrs. Trigg.

149

"Now what can it be?" And she began touching all the things on the shelf and looking at Robert. And when she touched the alarm-clock, he barked very loud, so she knew that was what he wanted. So Aunt Etta gave him the clock, and he carried it and the picture out on the porch and showed them to the other animals.

"Now," he said, "we've got an alarm-clock for Mr. Bean, Charles. You won't have to get up early in the morning any more when we get back." And Charles was very much pleased.

It was getting along toward supper-time by now, and all the farmers were climbing into their buggies and automobiles and driving away. They were happy to have recovered their valuables, and when somebody started to sing, they all joined in. Many of them sang part-songs all the way home. It was very inspiring.

Soon there was nobody left on the porch but Aunt Etta and her niece and Mrs. Trigg and a stout lady who lived across the road and whose name was Mrs. Hackenbutt.

"It does seem to me," said Aunt Etta, "that a photograph and an alarm-clock are a very small reward to give these animals for bringing back our things."

"Now we've got an alarm-clock for Mr. Bean."

"It isn't very much," agreed her niece, "but I can't think of anything else. Can you?"

"*I* can think of something," said Mrs. Hackenbutt suddenly. "We could help them to get all that dreadful paint off. I've been watching that cat and he's been licking himself for an hour. He wants to get it off. Now, if we could give them a good scrubbing——"

"That might do," said Aunt Etta. "I always say that there's nothing that good hot suds won't take out."

Now, if there is anything a cat hates more than cold water, it is hot water, and so Jinx immediately crawled under the porch and stayed there. Hank and Mrs. Wiggins would have liked to crawl under too, but of course they were too large. As for Robert and Freddy, they thought it was undignified to run away, so they sat nobly on the porch and waited while the women heated water in the washboiler and brought it out to them.

Then Mrs. Hackenbutt and Aunt Etta's niece rolled up their sleeves and set to work with scrubbing-brushes. They scrubbed and scrubbed, and pretty soon the thick paint began to loosen its hold on the animals' skins and peel off. "This isn't as bad as I thought it was going to be," said Mrs Wiggins.

"It's fine," said Hank. "I used to wonder why Mr. Bean took a bath every Saturday night, but I know now why he likes it so much."

When they had got off as much paint as they could, the women led the animals round to the pump and rinsed them off with buckets of cool well-water. But Jinx didn't come out until it was all over, and then he took care to keep out of sight.

They stayed at Aunt Etta's house that night, and would have liked to stay longer, but they knew that Mr. Bean needed them and thought they ought to start along. They hurried back to the log house in the woods and dug up the gold and put it in the phaeton.

"And now," said Freddy, "our adventures are over. Soon we'll be back in our own comfortable home again, and I for one shall be glad to be there."

"Yes," said Mrs. Wiggins, "our adventures are over for this year at least."

But she was wrong. For the most exciting adventure of all was lying in wait for them up the long, homeward road.

XVIII

NOTHING much happened, however, for the next few days. They plodded along the road, doing a steady twenty-five miles a day, for they were used to it now and could go much longer without getting tired than when they first set out. Most of the people they met had heard about them by this time, and although they attracted a good deal of attention, nobody molested them. The heap of gold coins lay in the bottom of the phaeton, but they had covered it up with the old shawl, so that no one knew that anything was there.

At last one morning they came to the bridge where the animals had found Mr. and Mrs. Webb again after they had fallen into the river. The two spiders were much excited, and Mrs. Webb ran up to the tip of Mrs. Wiggins's left horn, and Mr. Webb ran up to the tip of her right horn, and they sat there and looked out across the landscape and shouted to each other: "Oh, do you remember this?" and "Oh, do you remember that?" until Mrs. Webb was so overcome by the recollection of their strange adventure that she burst into tears. Then Mr. Webb climbed hurriedly down from Mrs. Wiggins's right horn and climbed up her left horn and patted his wife clumsily on the back with one of his eight feet, which he could also use as hands, and said: "There, there, Emmeline! Don't cry!" And Mrs. Webb wiped her eyes with a tiny pocket-handkerchief which she had woven herself, and stopped crying.

The animals went on across the bridge and through the village, and when they were out in the country again, Jack said: "I think, if nobody minds, I'd better ride in the carriage for a while. We're getting near to where I used to live, and I don't want the man I used to live with to see me. It might cause trouble."

Mrs. Wiggins gave a chuckle. "I have to laugh every time I think of that man, and the way he bounced like a rubber ball on the top of his automobile when I tossed him up there. He was an awful coward, even if he did have a big, black moustache."

"Yes," said Jack, as he climbed into the phaeton and crouched down under the shawl, "but just the same I think we'd better hurry along. He has a bad disposition, and he would take a lot of trouble to get even with us for the things we did to him."

"We mustn't take any chances with all this money," said Henrietta. So they hurried along, and pretty soon they passed the road which led up to the farm where the man with the black moustache lived, and then a little later they passed the swimming-hole in the river, where Mrs. Wiggins had fallen in.

"We ought to be pretty safe now," said Jack, "because he doesn't often come up this way in his automobile. But I'll stay in here for a while, just the same."

In another mile or two the road, which had been running across a valley, began to climb a long hill. It was getting along into the afternoon now, and as the animals had been walking fast, they were hot and dusty; so they were all glad when they came to a stream that crossed the road part way up the hill. They decided to take a swim.

"I remember this place," said Robert. "We stopped here to take a swim the day we started out, just before we met the man with the black moustache the first time."

"Yes, yes, so we did!" exclaimed the other animals. "Why, we're almost home! If we go on now we can get back to Mr. Bean's before midnight."

Some of them were all for going on at once when they realized how close home was, but Charles said: "We don't want to get there at night, when Mr. and Mrs. Bean and all the other animals are asleep. That won't be any fun!"

And Freddy said: "We'll be so tired when we get there that we won't want to tell them about our travels, and they'll be so sleepy that they won't want to hear about them. I vote we camp here to-night, and go on in the morning. We'll get home about dinner-time."

"That sounds sensible," said Hank. "We've come a long way to-day. If you ask me, I've had about enough. It's all right for you other animals, but I have to pull this carriage, and all that gold is heavier than Mr. and Mrs. Bean put together."

So they pulled the carriage under a tree, and pretty soon they were all splashing about in the water, which was pretty cold, for it was still early in the spring. But animals, with the exception of cats, do not mind cold water as much as some people do.

Now they were so near home, and so sure that nothing could interfere with their getting there, that they did not keep a very good watch while they were in swimming. And they did not see a pair of sharp eyes that were watching them from the bushes, nor hear the rustle of leaves as the bushes parted and the dirty-faced boy, who was the son of the man with the black moustache, sneaked over to the carriage and, lifting a corner of the shawl that covered the heap of gold coins, peeked under it. When they came back out of the water and ran up and down the bank to dry themselves, the boy had gone.

They did not sit up very late that night, for they were all pretty tired. Before they went to bed, Robert and Charles and Jack wound and set the alarm-clock. They had done this every night since Aunt Etta had given it to them. And this is the way they did it.

Jack held the clock in his mouth, and Robert took hold of the winder with his teeth, and they twisted. Sometimes it took them half an hour to do it, but they always did it. And when the clock part was wound up, they wound the alarm. But the thing you set the alarm with, to make it go off at a certain time in the morning, was so small that neither Robert nor Jack could get hold of it properly. And so when they had got it all wound, Charles would take hold of the thing with his beak and set it for whatever time they wanted to get up. This time they set it for five o'clock, because they wanted to get an early start.

They all took turns standing watch over the gold at night, and to-night it was Charles and Henrietta's turn. The other animals had found a warm and comfortable place to sleep under the little bridge, beside the stream, and when all good-nights had been said, the rooster and his wife made a final round of the camp to see that all was in order, and then flew up into the phaeton, perched on the back of the front seat, and tucked their heads under their wings.

They had not been asleep long when it began to rain. It rained gently at first, and Charles, half awakened, moved about a little on his perch, then dropped off again, lulled by the monotonous patter on the umbrella-like roof of the carriage. But the patter grew to a rattle, and then to a roar, and he awoke again to find his feathers getting wetter and wetter, and Henrietta tapping him crossly on the shoulder with her beak.

"Come, come, Charles; wake up!" she was saying. "We'll get wet and catch our deaths, very likely."

"This will never do!" said Charles. "We can't stay here. I think, my dear, we had better join the others under the bridge."

"I think we had better do nothing of the kind," said Henrietta crossly. "We are here to watch the gold, and here we stay. We can get down under the shawl in the back seat and keep dry. Come along."

"But the mice are sleeping here to-night," Charles protested. "And you know how Eeny snores. I shouldn't sleep a wink."

But Henrietta was not listening; she had jumped down into the back seat, and Charles followed her, repeating: "I shan't sleep a wink! Not a wink!" But once they had got under the shawl, where it was dry and warm, and had pushed the sleepy mice over to make room, he did fall asleep again with great promptness. It is true that Eeny snored, although it was not a very loud snore, for Eeny was a very small mouse. And then Cousin Augustus had the nightmare, and dreamed that four tortoise-shell cats with red eyes were chasing him, baying like the bloodhounds in *Uncle Tom's Cabin*, which he had once seen when he had been on a visit to his aunt, who lived in the town hall at Joy Centre, near Mr. Bean's farm. Cousin Augustus squeaked dreadfully when he had the nightmare, which was as often as he ate too much supper (and *that* was as often as he could)—and he jerked his legs and moaned and lashed his tail, so that Eek and Quik and Eeny had to get up and shake him awake. But even through all this Charles would have slept peacefully on if Henrietta had not pecked him on the neck and said: "Charles! Wake up! You'll have to do something about these mice. Keeping it up at all hours! I never heard such a racket! They don't seem to have any regard for anyone."

So Charles took his head out from under his wing. He couldn't see anything, because he was under the shawl, but he could hear Cousin Augustus waking up, and then saying: "Oh dear! Oh dear me! Such a dream! *Such* a dream!"

"Here, here!" said Charles sleepily, and trying to be stern. "What's all this? Do be still, can't you? Other people want to sleep if you don't!"

"Cousin Augustus had the nightmare," said Eek. "It's all over now."

Charles was satisfied with this and would have put his head back under his wing, but Henrietta pecked him again. So he said gruffly: "Well, we can't have that. Do you understand? We can't *have* it! We cannot have our rest broken in this way. I think you mice had better go and sleep somewhere else, as you don't seem able to do it quietly, like other animals."

The mice were a little afraid of Charles because he was so grand and talked so beautifully and strutted about the barn-yard so nobly, and so they did not give him any back talk, but climbed down meekly out of the carriage ond went to join the other animals under the bridge.

"Well, for once you had the gumption to stand up to somebody, even if it was only a mouse," said Henrietta. But Charles did not hear her, for he was again fast asleep.

There was now no sound under the shawl but the ticking of the alarm-clock and Charles's gentle breathing, and so Henrietta went to sleep too. When she awoke again, it was still dark. For a few minutes she could not tell what it was that had roused her; then she heard a faint creak, and the carriage gave a lurch to one side. It was moving! Something or somebody was drawing the carriage down the road!

She pecked Charles sharply, and he awoke with a groan. "Oh, my *goodness,* Henrietta! What is it *now?* Can't you let me alone?"

"Hush!" she whispered. "Don't you feel the carriage moving? Someone is running away with it. Someone's stealing the gold!"

Charles was very wide awake in an instant. He poked his head out from underneath the shawl and looked about him. Two shadowy forms—men, they looked like, though they might be animals— were pulling the carriage down the hill, and they must have pulled it some distance from where Hank had left it, for the bridge was nowhere in sight.

"This comes of not keeping watch," whispered Henrietta, who had poked her head out beside him.

"If you hadn't crawled under this shawl, you'd have been able to hear what was going on."

"You crawled under too," said Charles. "You're as much to blame as I am. But what shall we do? Even if I crow my loudest, they'll never hear me with the rain coming down the way it is."

"One of us must jump out and run back and give the alarm," said Henrietta. "And the other must stay here and find out where the carriage is being taken. You'd better go, Charles, and I'll stay."

Charles was too scared to complain at being ordered to go out in the heavy rain. The only thing he wanted was to get away from that carriage as quickly as possible. And being scared, he did what a scared rooster always does: he gave a loud squawk. And then he made a wild jump for the road. But his feet caught in the fringe of the shawl, and before he could get them free, and before Henrietta could get out herself, one of the dark figures dropped the handle of the carriage at which it was pulling, ran back, and caught them both. It was the dirty-faced boy.

"Hey! Pa!" he called. "Here's a couple nice chickens for Sunday dinner in here with the money."

They squawked and struggled, but he held on tight, and then the man with the black moustache came and tied their feet with string and shoved them roughly into the space under the front seat of the phaeton.

"I hope you're satisfied!" said Henrietta. "Of all the useless, good-for-nothing roosters, you're the worst! Why couldn't you keep your silly beak shut? My goodness, you certainly have got us in a nice mess now!" And she went on telling just what she thought of him. But Charles was not listening. "Sunday dinner," he was thinking, "Sunday dinner! Me, that's travelled hundreds and thousands of miles in my time—me, that's seen what I've seen and done what I've done, to end as a Sunday dinner! Fricasseed, probably, and eaten by perfect strangers!" And he burst into tears.

XIX

THE animals slept very soundly that night under the bridge, without a suspicion of the loss of their gold, or of the terrible fate that had overtaken Charles and Henrietta. Robert was the first to awake in the morning. It had stopped raining, but a heavy mist hid everything from sight.

"My goodness!" said Robert. "It must be dreadfully late! I wonder why I didn't hear the alarm when it went off at five o'clock. Hey, Freddy!" he called. "Hank! Wake up! We ought to have been on our way two hours ago."

In two minutes all the animals were wide awake, and Freddy had gone out to see what was the matter with the alarm-clock. Pretty soon he came running back. "The clock is gone," he panted, "and Charles and Henrietta are gone, and the phaeton is gone. Everything's gone. I bet Charles has run away with the treasure."

"Nonsense," said Mrs. Wiggins. "He couldn't if he wanted to. And besides, he isn't that kind of a rooster. I'm going out to see for myself."

The other animals followed her, and when they came to the place where the phaeton had been left, there was no phaeton there. But they found prints of muddy shoes all about the place, and the marks of the wheels in the muddy road were as plain as plain could be, so that they very soon knew what had happened.

"Charles and Henrietta were sleeping under the shawl," said Eek. "They made us get out. Probably they were captured in their sleep and didn't have a chance to call out to us."

"Here's one of Charles's tail feathers," cried Alice. "He wasn't captured without a struggle, you may be sure of that." She was a great admirer of Charles.

"We'd better start right away to follow these wheel marks," said Robert. "If we can find where the carriage has been taken to, maybe we can rescue them."

So they followed the marks on down the hill, and they led straight back the way the animals had come from Florida, until they came to the road that

"The clock is gone," he panted.

went down to the house where the man with the black moustache lived. And they turned down that road.

None of the animals said very much as they plodded along through the mist to the rescue of their friends. For they knew now that the man with the black moustache had stolen the carriage, and he was a dangerous and desperate character whom it would be hard to get the best of. Even Mr. Webb was worried. "He's a bad man," he said to his wife. "He'd squash a spider as soon as look at him." And Mrs. Webb shuddered.

Pretty soon they came near the house, and Jack said: "You'd better let me go ahead now, because I used to live here and I know my way round." So he led them by a back way round to where they could peek in the barn window, and sure enough, there was the phaeton, standing on the barn floor beside the rickety automobile. But the gold was not in it, and there was no sign of Charles and Henrietta.

Although the mist was so thick that they could not be seen from the house, they did not dare stay near the barn for fear that the man with the black moustache might come out and find them there. So the four mice said they would sneak up to the house and try to get in and find Charles and Henrietta, and the other animals went back and waited for them a little way down the road.

After quite a long time the mice came back, and the animals all crowded round them eagerly. "Did you see them?" they asked. "Are they all right? Did you find where the money is?"

"We didn't find out anything," said Eek. "We didn't even get into the house. I never saw such a house! Not a crack to get in by anywhere, and all the old mouse holes with pieces of tin nailed over them. We couldn't even get down the chimney, because there was a fire in the stove. He certainly is a mean man!"

"They're there, though," said Quik, "because we heard them talking. And Charles is there too, because we heard him crying."

"Poor thing" said Mrs. Wiggins. "But we'll get him out, if we have to tear the whole house down with our horns and claws and beaks and hoofs! Won't we, animals?"

"We will! We certainly will!" cried the determined travellers.

"But the first thing," she continued, "is to find

out where Charles and Henrietta are, and the second thing is to find where the money is; then we can make a plan. Has anybody anything to suggest?"

"I want to suggest something," shouted Mr. Webb. But nobody heard him. So he crawled down into Mrs. Wiggins's ear and stamped around until he tickled her, and then told her, and she told the others. He had an idea that he could get into the house through a keyhole, if Robert would carry him up to the door.

This seemed a good idea to everyone except Mrs. Webb, who thought it too dangerous. Indeed, she burst into tears at the very thought. "No, no, Hubert," she sobbed. "I can't let you go. You said yourself he was a wicked man. Suppose he should see you and hit you with a newspaper or something. I should never forgive myself if I let you go."

Mr. Webb, however, was firm in his decision, as spiders are apt to be, and, having kissed his weeping wife tenderly on the forehead, he jumped down on to Robert's back and they started.

At the front door he got down, and while Robert hid behind a bush to wait for him, he crawled up and squeezed in through the keyhole. It was gloomy inside, because the windows were rather dirty, but that didn't bother Mr. Webb, and he walked up the wall as easily as you would walk up your own front steps, and then he walked across the ceiling to the front parlour, where he heard voices.

The reason he walked on the ceiling was because that was the safest place for him to be. He knew that on the walls or the floor he was much more likely to be seen, but people hardly ever look up at the ceiling except when they are in bed. And then, too, if you see a spider on the floor, it is easy to run over and step on him, but that is a pretty difficult thing to do if he is on the ceiling.

So Mr. Webb walked boldly into the front parlour on the ceiling. The man with the black moustache and the dirty-faced boy were sitting at a table counting the gold coins they had stolen from the animals. They would count twenty, and then they would wrap them up in a piece of newspaper and pack them away in a big canvas bag. But they didn't get on very fast because they both counted out loud, and they kept mixing each other up and having to start all over again. Mr. Webb watched them for a while; then, hearing a noise in the far corner of the room, he walked over and saw Charles and Henrietta lying, with their feet tied, in a box beside the stove. Charles was lying on his back and staring gloomily at the ceiling, but Henrietta was picking busily with her beak at the knots in the string, and Mr. Webb saw that she had very nearly got herself loose.

All at once Charles caught sight of the spider. "Hey!" he shouted. "Mr. Webb! Oh, my golly, I'm glad to see you! How did you find us? Are the others all here?"

"What's the matter with those chickens?" said the boy. "Do you suppose one of 'em's laid an egg?"

"Eighteen, nineteen, twenty—it'll be the last egg it ever lays, then," said the man with a coarse laugh. "Day after to-morrow's Sunday," he added meaningly.

Mr. Webb hurried down the wall and climbed to the edge of the box. "For goodness' sake, Charles, keep still!" he whispered. "Henrietta, do you think you can get those strings off?"

Henrietta nodded without stopping her work.

"Very good, then," said Mr. Webb. "Get them loose enough so that you can get out of them quickly, but don't take them off, because it might be noticed. And I'll see what I can do. Cheer up, Charles," he added, slapping the unhappy rooster heartily on the back. "We won't desert you."

On the wall, in a gilt frame, was a large picture of a man with a grey moustache, who was the father of the man with the black moustache and the grandfather of the dirty-faced boy. Mr. Webb walked down into the darkness behind this picture, and sat down cross-legged on the dusty picture wire and tried to think of a plan. But though he thought of a good many, there was just one thing the matter with all of them—they wouldn't work.

"I'm wasting precious time here," he thought. "I'd better go back and tell the animals and let them try to think of something, since I can't." And he started up the wire toward the ceiling.

But just at the edge of the picture frame he caught sight of a fly. The fly was sound asleep. It had had a very hearty breakfast that morning of jelly and cream and egg that the man with the black moustache had spilled on the table-cloth at *his* breakfast, and it had flown up on to the picture frame to take a little nap before going down to lunch on more jelly and cream and egg.

Mr. Webb, however, had not had any breakfast, so he crept up quietly behind the fly and grabbed it by the leg. The fly buzzed and struggled, but Mr. Webb held on, and then it stopped struggling and said: "O, Mr. Spider—good, *kind* Mr. Spider, please let me go. Please don't eat me. If you won't eat me, I'll do anything you want me to."

Now most spiders would not have paid any attention, but would have gobbled the fly up then and there. But Mr. Webb had a very kind heart, and married life had further softened him, so that he paused. And while he was pausing, a thought came to him.

"If you'll give me your word to do exactly as I tell you," he said, "I'll let you go. What's more, I'll go away out of this house and won't come back again. But if you don't do it, then I and my wife and all my relations will come and live in this house and eat you all up."

The fly promised, and Mr. Webb let him go. "Now," he said, "you go out and get all your relations and neighbours and meet me in the hall, and I'll tell you what I want you to do."

So the fly slipped outdoors through the keyhole in the front door, and pretty soon he came back, and with him were all his family and neighbours. Young flies and stout, middle-aged flies and old grandfather flies with no teeth and old grandmother flies with the rheumatism in their wings—they came pouring in through the keyhole and formed in a wide circle around Mr. Webb on the hall ceiling. And Mr. Webb made a long speech and explained the situation and told them just what they were to do. And immediately they started in to do it.

First they flew into the front parlour and lit on the ceiling. Then when Mr. Webb saw that Henrietta had untied the last knot and had got Charles's feet as well as her own free, he said: "Go!" And the flies jumped into the air and began whirling round the room, buzzing as loud as they could. And the youngest and most active ones pestered the man and the boy. Two or three of them would light on the man's nose and dance round with all six feet so as to tickle as much as possible. And when he raised nis hand to brush them off, they would fly over and tickle the back of the boy's neck. In a few minutes both the man and the boy were pretty nearly crazy. They stopped counting coins, and folded up newspapers and tried to slap the flies, but as soon as they did that, all the flies would go up to the ceiling. And then as soon as they laid the newspapers down, the flies would start in again.

"Phoo!" said the man. "Whoosh! Get away, you things! I don't see where they come from. There wasn't one here five minutes ago."

"It's no good trying to swat them," said the boy. "Poof! Get out of my ear! They seem to be trying to get out of the window. Let's open it, and maybe they'll go out."

The man looked at the window, where forty or fifty flies were walking round on the glass. "If it weren't for those animals, I'd open it," he said. "But I'm afraid they'll be round here somewhere after their gold. They're a pretty smart set of animals, and I shan't feel safe until we have taken the gold into the village to-morrow morning, and put it in the bank. You remember what they did to us last fall."

"I'd rather have forty animals in here than all these flies," said the boy. "Besides, we can watch, and if we see them coming, we can slam the window down again." And he went and unlocked the window and threw it open, and stood beside it to put it down again when all the flies were out.

But although the flies streamed out by tens and

dozens, as soon as they got outside, they went round to the front door and came in again through the keyhole, as Mr. Webb had instructed them to. So that although they had stopped bothering, there seemed to be just as many in the room as there were before. And for every dozen that flew out of the window, twelve came in through the keyhole.

"My goodness," said the boy, "there's no end to them."

"Well, we'll have to leave the window open, that's all," said the man. "Come, sit down and let's get these coins counted." And they started counting again, keeping a sharp look-out on the window.

Now, this was just what Mr. Webb had hoped they would do, and he motioned to Charles and Henrietta, who had been peering anxiously over the edge of the box. The man and the boy were watching the window, so that they did not see their two prisoners climb cautiously out of the box and tiptoe toward them. Charles was almost dead with fright, but he followed Henrietta until they stood just under the table. And then, at a signal from Mr. Webb, the flies all whirled down and began walking up and down the man's nose and buzzing in the boy's ears and generally plaguing them twice as much as they had before. And while they waved their arms to drive the flies off, and shut their eyes to keep the flies out of them, Charles and Henrietta hopped on the window-sill and down on the grass outside, and than ran for their lives.

Then Mr. Webb went out into the hall and the flies gathered round him, and he made them a little speech of thanks, and then dismissed them. As he foilowed the last fly out through the keyhole, he heard the parlour window go shut with a bang, and then the boy called: "Hey, pa! Pa! Look, pa! The chickens are gone!"

He chuckled to himself. "That's a good job done," he said. "But now how are we going to get the gold?"

XX

YOU may believe that Charles and Henrietta were glad to see their friends again, and that their friends were glad to see them. Charles shook hands with the dogs and Freddy and Hank and the mice, and Henrietta kissed the ducks and Mrs. Wiggins. She almost put Mrs. Wiggins's eye out with her beak. Then she would have kissed Mrs. Webb, but Mrs. Webb begged to be excused.

"Now, animals," said Robert, "we've got to hold a council of war. We've got to get that gold, and we've got to get it before to-morrow morning, because Henrietta says they intend to take it into the village and put it in the bank to-morrow, and if they do that, we'll never see it again."

"We've got to get into the house somehow," said Jinx, "and it must be after dark, when they can't see us get in. So the flies can't help us any; they'll

179

all be asleep. Now, how can we make them open a window or a door?"

"Mr. Bean always opens a window for fresh air when he goes to bed," said Hank.

"You can take my word for it, this man doesn't do that," said Henrietta. "I never smelt such a stuffy house in my life."

"Mr. Bean spilt some grease on the stove once," said Robert, "and she opened the window to let the smoke out."

"Yes, but we can't get in to put anything on the stove," said Eek.

"Wait a minute," said Jinx suddenly. "That gives me an idea. Yes, I know how we can work it," he said excitedly. And he explained his plan, which, as you will see later, was a pretty clever one, even for a cat to think of.

Nothing could be done until late that night, so for the rest of the day the animals sat round in the woods, keeping well out of sight of the house. They tried to play games to pass away the time, but home was so near, and they were all so anxious to get there, and so impatient of the delay, that the games didn't seem much fun. But at last the sun went down and the long shadows crept out of the woods and hid the grass and trees, and the stars began to wink and twinkle in the dark-blue sky. Even then the animals did not start to carry out their plan, and it was not until about nine o'clock, when the light in the house had gone out and they knew that the man and the boy had gone to bed, that Jinx said it was time to go.

Then they all went into a field that was near the house, and Freddy with his sharp nose and Hank with the toes of his iron shoes tore up by the roots a good-sized heap of grass. This they carried up close to the house, and then Jinx took as much as he could carry and climbed up the back porch on to the roof and dropped it down the chimney. Then he went down and carried up another piece, and he kept on doing this until the chimney was all plugged up.

Inside the house the man and the boy were sound asleep, with the bag of gold by the head of their bed. Fortunately for the animals, they had made up a big fire in the stove so that they wouldn't have to build a new one in the morning, and pretty soon the smoke that couldn't get up through the chimney began to pour out into the front parlour. And from the front parlour it went into the hall and up the stairs, and at last into the bedroom. And then it got into the boy's throat and woke him up.

"Fire!" he yelled, jumping out of bed. "Fire! Wake up, pa! The house is on fire!"

In a minute they were both up and rushing down the stairs in their white night-shirts, dragging the heavy bag of gold after them. Bump, bump, clink, jingle it went. They unlocked the front door and rushed out into the yard, and there they dropped the bag and sat down on it, panting. Then they looked up at the house.

"Why, the house isn't afire!" said the man.

"Where does the smoke come from then?" asked the boy.

"I don't know," said his father. "Must be a fire somewhere. We'd better go back and see." So they dragged the bag of gold back into the house, but they left the front door open behind them in case the fire should break out suddenly.

The animals, who had been hiding behind trees and bushes, now crept up closer to the door, and as soon as they heard the man and the boy moving round in the front parlour, they tiptoed into the house. Jinx and the mice hurried upstairs into the bedroom, and while Jinx carried the two pairs of

shoes into another room and hid them under a
bureau, the mice gnawed all the buttons off the
clothes. Freddy and Robert and Jack hid under
the dining-room table, and Hank hid most of himself behind the long velvet curtains at the dining-
room window, although his head and tail showed.
They made a good deal of noise getting in, but the
man and the boy were talking excitedly and throw-
ing up windows to let the smoke out, and didn't
hear them. Even when Mrs. Wiggins knocked over
the umbrella-stand in the hall, they didn't notice it.

When the animals were all in the house and Mrs.
Wiggins had lain down in a corner of the dining-
room with a red table-cloth thrown over her so as
to look as much as possible like a piece of furniture,
Jinx came to the head of the stairs and began to
make noises. A cat can make terrible noises when
he really tries, and Jinx was really trying. He
moaned and groaned and howled and yowled, and
in a minute the man and the boy came out into the
hall. They were very much frightened, and the
animals could see that their knees were shaking
under the edges of their night-shirts.

"Oh, pa!" said the boy. "Wh-wh-what is that?"

"Here," said the man. "You take this bag or gold into the dining-room and watch it. I'm going up to see." And he started up the stairs.

The boy dragged the bag into the dining-room and shut the door. All the animals stood perfectly still, and as there wasn't much light in the room, although it was bright moonlight outside, he didn't see them. But he did see Mrs. Wiggins.

"Why, where'd this red sofa come from?" he said aloud. "I never saw that before." And he went over and sat down on her.

Now Mrs. Wiggins had a sense of humour. That means that she always laughed at the wrong time. And she began to laugh now.

"Yow!" yelled the boy, and he jumped up, and, forgetting all about the bag of gold that he had been told to watch, he ran upstairs to tell his father that the sofa in the dining-room was alive.

And at that moment Robert came out from underneath the table. "Now's our chance, animals," he said. And Mrs. Wiggins threw off the table-cloth, and Hank came out from behind the curtains, and Freddy and Jack came from under the table, and they all grabbed hold of the heavy bag with their teeth and heaved and dragged and pulled it out into the hall, and through the front door, and across the yard to the barn. As quickly as they could, they hoisted it into the phaeton, and Hank took the ropes over his shoulders and pulled the carriage out into the yard. Jinx and the mice had sneaked downstairs again while the man was looking through the bedrooms, and they climbed aboard with Charles and Henrietta and the ducks.

"All ready, Hank," said Robert. "We're all here. Next stop is Home. One, two, three—*go!*" And away they went out of the gate and up the road with a rattle of flying stones, as fast as Hank could gallop, with the dogs and Freddy running alongside, and Mrs. Wiggins thundering along behind, while all the smaller animals hung on for dear life with beaks and bills and claws.

Now, the man had not found anything upstairs, and he began to suspect that a trick had been played on him. When he heard the rattle of wheels and the thud of flying hoofs, he was sure of it. He didn't say anything then to the boy for leaving the gold unguarded; he would give him his licking for that later, he thought. He rushed downstairs to

185

the dining-room, and sure enough, the bag was gone. Then he ran to the door, just in time to see the last part of Mrs. Wiggins going through the gate.

"Get your clothes on!" he yelled to the boy, giving him a cuff on the ear. "It's the animals. I might have known it! But we can catch them if we hurry. They forgot that we had an automobile."

Now it was easy enough for them to get their clothes on, but it wasn't at all easy to keep them on, for the mice had gnawed all the buttons off. They worked and worked at them for a long time, and finally had to fasten them together with pins. And that didn't work very well either, for every time they moved, the pins stuck into them and made them yell. Then when they were all ready, they couldn't find their shoes at all, so they went out finally in their stocking-feet, and cranked up their rickety old automobile and started in pursuit.

By this time the animals had got a pretty good start. But as they began to climb the hill on the other side of the valley, they looked over their shoulders, and far off down the road they could see the two little lights of the pursuing automobile growing bigger and bigger, and they could hear, plainer and plainer, the rattle and pop of the engine, as the man with the black moustache drove furiously on their trail.

"I don't know as we'll make it," panted Hank.

"We've *got* to make it," said Robert. "Keep going for all you're worth."

But as they went on, it grew plainer and plainer that they couldn't make it, for the automobile was travelling twice as fast as they were. And just as they got to the bridge where they had slept the night before, Hank slowed down to a walk.

"It's no use," he said. "I can't run up this hill. Can't we turn off and hide in the woods?"

"Not with a carriage," said Mrs. Wiggins. "But Hank, you go on, and I'll stay here on the bridge and keep them back. Go as fast as you can, and I'll overtake you if I can before you get home. And wait: I want the mice to stay, too. I think they can help."

At first the animals wouldn't consent to leave her behind. "We'll stay and fight it out beside you," they said. But she said no, she had a good plan, and they'd only spoil it if they stayed. So they

187

said good-bye sorrowfully, and went on, leaving Mrs. Wiggins and the mice to hold the bridge.

As soon as they were gone, Mrs. Wiggins set to work. She pushed down the railings at the side of the bridge with her horns and tore up some of the boards and piled them all in the middle. Then she and the mice sat down behind a bush and waited. Pretty soon the automobile came bounding up the hill, rattling as if it would fall to pieces the next minute. And at every bound the man and the boy let out a great yell as the pins with which their clothes were fastened together stuck into them.

Just in time the man saw the pile of boards, and he slammed on the brakes and stopped so quickly that he and his son flew right out over the front and landed sitting down on the bridge. And at once they let out a piercing yell, for all the pins had stuck into them at the same time. Then they got up and began clearing away the boards.

"Now, mice," whispered Mrs. Wiggins, "out with you, and do as I told you." And the mice crept out, and each one of them climbed up on a tire, and they set to work with their sharp little teeth to nibble holes through the hard rubber.

"Pretty tough gnawing," squeaked Eeny.

"Keep at it, brothers," chirped Quik. "Everything depends on us now."

But the tires were very hard, and before any of them had made deep enough holes to let the air out, the boards were cleared away and the man started up his engine. Then the mice had to jump down, and Mrs. Wiggins got up and lowered her head and shook her horns and prepared to charge at the enemy. But just as the automobile started slowly across the bridge, and just as she was about to gallop out and try to tumble it over into the water below—pingggg! went the left front tire, and fizz-wizz-wizz-wizz! went the right front tire, and the other two tires blew up with a bang, and the automobile wobbled and came to a standstill. For though the mice hadn't gnawed all the way through the tires, they had weakened them so that they gave way as soon as the automobile started.

Then the man with the black moustache knew that his chance was gone, and that he couldn't overtake the animals and get back the gold. For quite a little while he stood staring mournfully up the road. But he was a practical man, which means that he believed in doing *something* immediately, even if it wasn't anything very useful. So he picked up a piece of board and took the dirty-faced boy across his knee and gave him a good licking. And then he turned round and walked home in his stocking-feet.

XXI

EARLY the next morning the head of Mr. Bean, the farmer, appeared at his bedroom window. The fresh morning breeze swung the red tassel of his white cotton night-cap and waved his bushy, grey whiskers. He was looking out to see what kind of a day it was going to be.

"My goodness!" said Mr. Bean. "It's nearly six o'clock! I certainly do miss that rooster! I haven't been up on time one single morning since he left."

He dressed quickly and went downstairs and out into the cow barn and gave Mrs. Wurzburger and Mrs. Wogus their breakfasts, and then he fed the chickens and the pigs and William, the horse, and the other animals. Jock, the wise old collie, went along with him.

Pretty soon Mrs. Bean rang the breakfast bell, and he went in and sat down at the table and tucked his napkin under his chin and had coffee and pancakes and hot biscuit and ham and eggs and oatmeal and two kinds of jam. And when he had had enough, he pushed back his chair and lit his pipe, taking care not to set fire to his whiskers with the match.

Then he said: "Mrs. Bean, I don't know how you feel about it, but I certainly should like to have those animals back again. It seems sort of lonesome here this nice spring weather without Robert and Hank and Mrs. Wiggins and all the rest of them."

"Mr. Bean," said his wife, "I have heard you say that every morning after breakfast since the animals went away. And I will reply as I always reply: I miss them too, especially Jinx. He was a nice cat."

"I've sometimes thought," said Mr. Bean, "that maybe they wouldn't have gone away if I had been nicer to them."

"You was always a kind man to your animals, Mr. Bean," his wife replied.

"Yes," he said. "I try to be. I gave them plenty to eat and didn't work them too hard, but after all I didn't make them as comfortable as I might. All their houses needed repairing, and they were pretty draughty and cold in the winter-time."

"Well, we didn't have the money to fix them up," said his wife.

"That's true. That's true," said Mr. Bean with a sigh. And for some time neither of them said anything.

Then all at once, out in the barn-yard, Jock began to bark and the hens began to cackle and the cows mooed and the ducks quacked and the pigs squealed; and Mr. Bean jumped up and ran to the window. "What on earth is the matter?" he exclaimed, and then: "Wife! Wife!" he cried. "Here they are! Here are the animals back! Come out! Come out into the yard!" And out they rushed to welcome the wanderers.

All the animals who had stayed at home lined up on either side of the gate to welcome them. First came Charles and Henrietta, wing in wing, and then came Jinx, proudly waving his red tail, and then Freddy and Jack and Robert. And behind them came the phaeton, drawn by Hank. And Mrs. Wiggins, with Alice and Emma and the four mice on her back, brought up the rear. They marched in the gate and went three times around

the barn-yard, while the animals and Mr. and Mrs.
Bean cheered themselves hoarse. And then they
stopped the phaeton directly in front of Mr. Bean,
and Robert jumped into it and, with the help of
Jack and Mrs. Wiggins, tumbled the bag of gold
out on the ground.

"What on earth!" Mr. Bean exclaimed, and he
bent down and untied the bag, and out rolled a
stream of bright yellow coins. "Gold!" he cried.
"Twenty-dollar gold pieces! Why, here's thousands of dollars! Enough to build twenty new
barns if we want 'em! And you brought all this
back to me!" He stood motionless for a minute,
and then he snatched off his night-cap (which he
still had on), and threw it up in the air and grabbed
Mrs. Bean round the waist and waltzed her around
the barn-yard until they were both so dizzy they
had to stop. And all the animals cheered and
danced round too. Then Mr. and Mrs. Bean went
round and hugged all the animals, even the mice,
who were very happy, but scared all the same to be
hugged so hard. And when the alarm-clock and
the shawl and the other things they had brought
back with them had been admired, Mr. Bean made
a speech.

"Animals and friends," he said, "I thank you a thousand times for this magnificent and munificent gift. Had you brought me back nothing but yourselves, I should have been more than happy, but since you have brought me wealth as well, I intend that you shall share in its benefits. You shall have new homes, fitted with all the modern conveniences. The workmen shall start on them to-morrow, and Mrs. Bean and I will draw the plans for them to-night. Those of you who work regularly shall work in the future no more than six hours a day, and when, as is sometimes necessary, either Hank or William works longer than that, he shall have an extra measure of oats, with sugar, for each hour of overtime. Since I have an alarm-clock, Charles may sleep as late as he wishes in the morning. I will have electric lights strung up over the duck pond, as well as in the various houses, and a small house will also be built for the mice. And perhaps next winter we can all go south together.

"And now, my friends, you are no doubt anxious to greet your relatives and talk over your adventures by flood and field; so to-day we will do no more work, but will celebrate it as a holiday in honour of your home-coming. No doubt, too, you are hungry, and Mrs. Bean will go in and prepare a feast for you, while I set to work on the plans for your new quarters. Again I thank you, my friends, from the bottom of my heart."

That night, when the celebration was over, and the animals had all gone to bed, Freddy, the pig, who had eaten a great deal more than was good for him and consequently did not feel like sleeping, walked out into the moonlight.

"After all," he said to himself, "it's exciting to travel and have adventures, but there's no place like home." And he looked affectionately at the old familiar pig pen, where so many happy hours had been spent. And then he made up this song:

> Oh, a life of adventure is gay and free,
>   And danger has its charm;
> And no pig of spirit will bound his life
>   By the fence on his master's farm.

> Yet there's no true pig but heaves a sigh
> At the pleasant thought of the old home sty.

But one tires at last of wandering,
  And the road grows steep and long,
A treadmill round, where no peace is found,
  If one follows it overlong.

And however they wander, both pigs and
    men
Are always glad to get home again.